NEMESIS

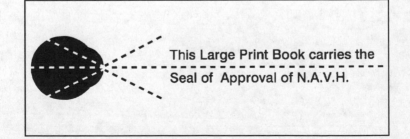

This Large Print Book carries the
Seal of Approval of N.A.V.H.

A NAMELESS DETECTIVE NOVEL

NEMESIS

BILL PRONZINI

THORNDIKE PRESS
A part of Gale, Cengage Learning

Detroit • New York • San Francisco • New Haven, Conn • Waterville, Maine • London

Copyright © 2013 by the Pronzini-Muller Family Trust.
Thorndike Press, a part of Gale, Cengage Learning.

Thorndike Press® Large Print Mystery.
The text of this Large Print edition is unabridged.
Other aspects of the book may vary from the original edition.
Set in 16 pt. Plantin.

LIBRARY OF CONGRESS CATALOGING-IN-PUBLICATION DATA

Pronzini, Bill.
   Nemesis : a Nameless Detective novel / by Bill Pronzini. — Large print edition.
      pages ; cm. — (Thorndike Press large print mystery)
   ISBN-13: 978-1-4104-6166-7 (hardcover)
   ISBN-10: 1-4104-6166-1 (hardcover)
   1. Nameless Detective (Fictitious character)—Fiction. 2. Private investigators—Fiction. 3. Extortion—Fiction. 4. Large type books. I. Title.
PS3566.R67N43 2013b
813'.54—dc23   2013023545

Published in 2013 by arrangement with Tom Doherty Association, LLC

Printed in the United States of America
1 2 3 4 5 6 7 17 16 15 14 13

For Mike White, with thanks once again for his essential advice on matters of police procedure and criminal law

PROLOGUE

Difficult times, painful times.

Kerry wasn't the same after what happened to her in Green Valley in the Sierra foothills.

A thing like that, the unrelenting terror of it, takes a heavy physical and mental toll on everybody involved. I'd suffered through it, too, as had Jake Runyon, but Jake and I were thick-skinned, case-hardened veterans of crises and near-fatal experiences — in my case a similar abduction and lengthy confinement years ago. We were able to shed the worst of the effects in fairly short order, regain what passes for a normal state of mind in men like us. But what we'd gone through those four horrific days in early July was nothing compared to what Kerry had endured at the hands of the psychotic named Balfour.

She'd faced her ordeal, and the ten days in the hospital that followed her rescue, with the same heroic courage, resiliency, and determination with which she'd survived breast cancer. Only this time she'd come a lot closer to dying an even more terrible death, and the psychological damage had been profound. Her physical wounds healed and left no discernible scars, but even after more than two months, her emotions were as raw and festering as flesh exposed beneath flayed skin.

Those four days in July had robbed her — short-term, I prayed to God — of all the qualities that made her the strong woman she'd been before.

And left her fearful.

Ever since I'd brought her home from the hospital, she refused to leave the condo by herself. Was reluctant to go out in public even if I was with her, and avoided people she knew the handful of times I was able to talk her into it. The only person aside from Emily and me that she'd deal with face-to-face was her mother at the seniors' complex in Larkspur where she lived. Cybil, elderly and frail, had not been spared the knowledge of Kerry's ordeal because of the media attention it had caused, and her health had further deteriorated as a result. That, too, contributed to Kerry's fearfulness.

She had trouble sleeping. Nightmares that

she wouldn't talk about plagued her when she did drop off. More than once she cried out in the late-night darkness, and twice screamed loud enough to wake both of us.

She'd lost weight, grown thin and gaunt. She had no appetite — shunned food half the time, only picked at it when Emily and I succeeded in convincing her to eat. Her fondness for wine disappeared; she wouldn't take so much as a sip. That, at least, was something of a relief: too many others in her fragile emotional condition tried to find solace in alcohol.

At odd moments — at the dinner table, while reading or watching TV — she would suddenly burst into tears, then rush away to lock herself in her office. She spent most of her waking hours closeted in there. That was all right up to a point; the one piece of normalcy she'd been able to recapture was her ability to work. Except that what amounted to an escape mechanism seemed to grow into a kind of mania. She spent ten, twelve hours a day at her computer, directing ad campaigns, writing copy, interfacing with the other upper management people at Bates and Carpenter.

Most of the time she didn't want to be touched by either Emily or me, not even so much as a hug or peck on the cheek. But every now and then, late at night, I would wake up to find her body fitted tight against mine, her arms and legs wrapped around me, clinging so fiercely it was as if she were trying to crawl inside my skin.

Nothing helped much. Not a handful of sessions with a crisis counselor and a psychologist her doctor recommended; she talked to them freely enough, or so she claimed, but didn't seem to take anything beneficial from the sessions. Not prescription tranquilizers or sleeping pills. Not the comfort and reassurance offered by friends and coworkers, and by Emily and me daily. It wasn't that she was apathetic; she tried as hard as she could. It was just that she was "temporarily lost inside herself," as the doctor phrased it.

Despite the negligible progress, I kept telling her — and Emily and myself — that the medical people were right and the condition was only temporary; that the old time-heals bromide was true. I believed it. So did Emily — a rock during all of this, so much more mature than her fourteen years, never complaining, always upbeat and supportive. But did Kerry believe it?

Time. Time. Give it enough and she'd find her way back.

I did not return to work myself. Kerry said

I should, but it was lip-service encouragement; it was obvious she felt more secure when I was close by. I wouldn't have returned in any case. For my own peace of mind I had to be there for her in case she needed me. And I knew I wouldn't be able to concentrate on complex or even routine investigative matters; I'd have been more of a liability than an asset to the agency.

I had a long talk with Tamara about my decision. She understood and accepted it without question. She and Jake and Alex Chavez could handle the caseload as it stood now; if it grew too heavy, she'd bring back Deron Stewart and if necessary hire yet another part-time field operative. We could afford the extra expense — business had never been better, despite and in certain cases because of the lousy economy. Meanwhile I'd be available for consultation by phone or for the kind of simple tasks I could perform using my limited computer skills.

We called it a leave of absence, but that was only a convenient euphemism. Even when Kerry found herself again — when, not if — I was not so sure I wanted to climb back into harness on the former semi-retired, part-time basis. It might be better for everybody if I phased myself out of the operation completely. Kerry was not the only one who had been stripped bare in Green Valley. I'd lost some of my courage and resilience and determination up there, too.

Difficult times, painful times.

■ ■ ■ ■

PART ONE:
JAKE RUNYON

■ ■ ■ ■

1

The address Tamara had given him for Verity Daniels's condo was one of the big, new SoMa high-rises on Harrison, just off the Embarcadero. Which meant that Ms. Daniels had money and plenty of it, one of the reasons, if not the main reason, that Tamara had agreed to an after–business hours appointment to accommodate a prospective client. You couldn't buy into a place like Bayfront Towers unless you had a minimum of a quarter of a million to spend on lodging.

Runyon didn't have to try to find street parking, which would've been next to impossible in South Beach at 5:30 on a weekday: too many restaurants and clubs, and the Giants playing a late-afternoon game at AT&T Park down at China Basin. Bayfront Towers had an underground garage with visitor parking. But you couldn't just leave your car and take an elevator up to the residents' units unannounced; you had to go through security protocol first.

A uniformed security man in the garage had Runyon's name and the fact that he was expected by Ms. Daniels — that was the first step. Then he was directed to take an elevator that only went up as far as the lobby; the other garage elevator was for residents only, operated either by key or keycard. In the lobby there was a glassed-in cubicle full of monitoring equipment and another uniformed guard presiding over it. Runyon had to sign a logbook before he was allowed access to the visitor's elevator. Modern urban living in steel-and-glass luxury. All well and good for those who could afford it and felt comfortable with it. For him it would have been like living inside a fortified watchtower — living scared.

The high-speed elevator whisked him up to the twelfth floor, deposited him in a carpeted hallway with indirect lighting and pieces of decorative furniture that no one would ever sit in. Muted chimes sounded inside condo 1206 when he pressed an inlaid pearl button. There was a peephole in the door; he felt himself being scrutinized even though he'd been announced by the desk guard, had opened the leather case containing his license photostat, and held it

16

up to the glass eye. Even so, it was half a minute before chain and bolt locks were released and the door opened.

"I'm Verity Daniels, Mr. Runyon. Thank you for being so prompt. Please come in."

Thirty or so, large-boned and on the voluptuous side. Dark hair cut in a short, feathery, in-curling style, mild blue eyes under artfully plucked and arched brows, a wide mouth painted with too much lipstick, a beauty mark just above the angle of her chin. Runyon was no expert when it came to women's clothes, but he knew expensive silk when he saw it: the silvery gray jacket and skirt and darker colored blouse with gold buttons must have had a four-figure price tag. Likewise the diamond-chip earrings, the blood-ruby ring on the little finger of her right hand, the thin platinum gold watch on her left wrist. An expensive packaging job, and yet the effect didn't seem quite natural. As if she weren't used to all the rich woman's trappings, wasn't completely comfortable with the image she presented.

The place, a large studio rather than a full-sized apartment, gave him the same impression. Richly furnished in blond wood, modern art on a couple of the walls, thick, pale blue carpeting, matching blue drapes drawn back over picture windows that provided an off-angle view of the bay, the Bay Bridge and Treasure Island, the East Bay hills. The only thing that didn't quite fit the decor was a huge flat-screen TV mounted on another wall. The rest carried the carefully planned, formalized stamp of an interior decorator, and all of it looked brand new, unlived in: no personal touches, nothing out of place. He wondered if Ms. Daniels was afraid of disturbing its showroom perfection. If she wasn't at home in surroundings like these, why choose to live in them?

She seemed to think his casual inspection was centered on the flat-screen. "I watch a lot of TV," she said, but not as if embarrassed by the fact. "It's really too big for the room, isn't it? The television?"

To be polite he said, "Looks okay to me."

She invited him to sit on one of a pair of streamlined chairs, claimed the other across a kidney-shaped, glass-topped table. She sat primly, knees together, hands folded in her lap. Runyon set his briefcase on the floor and readied his notebook while he waited for her to open the conversation. Took her close to a minute, but not because she was having difficulty finding words, he thought. She spent the silent period studying him, her eyes unblinking, a faint half smile appearing and disappearing on her too-red mouth. Measuring him, trying to decide how competent and trustworthy he was, maybe. He'd been subjected to that kind of client scrutiny before.

But that wasn't quite it, because when she finally spoke it was to say, "You know, I've seen your name in the newspaper. You must be a very good detective."

There was nothing for him to say to that. He shrugged, smiled a little, waited.

"Have you been one long? A detective?"

"Fourteen years with the Seattle police. Nearly eight as a private investigator."

"It must be exciting work."

"Sometimes. Mostly it's routine."

"Oh, I'm sure you're just being modest."

He let that pass, too. Get to the point, he was thinking, but he kept waiting in attentive silence. You had to let these interviews develop in their own way. She figured to be nervous, a little on edge in spite of her outward show of calm.

Pretty soon she gave herself a little shake and said, "Well. Would you like something to drink? Coffee? Tea? A soda? I'm afraid I can't offer you anything stronger. I don't drink alcohol, so I don't keep any on hand."

"Nothing, thanks."

19

"Well," she said again. "It really is good of you to come at this hour. Ms. Corbin said you wouldn't mind, given my busy schedule, but I know it must be an imposition. . . ."

"Not at all."

She seemed to feel the need to explain further, in more detail than was necessary. "You see, I inherited quite a large sum of money six months ago from my aunt — she was an actress who lived in Paris, famous on the European stage. I had no idea she was so wealthy or that she'd leave me as much as she did. Well, anyway, I no longer need to work for a living, so I've become rather heavily involved in charity work. Fund-raising for Lighthouse for the Blind, Foundation for AIDS Research, the Breast Cancer Fund. The problems they deal with are so much more important than mine and I hate to take time away from my work for them."

Runyon nodded. The recent inheritance explained the newness of the studio and her lack of ease in dress and surroundings. Nouveau riche. Brand-new lifestyle.

"Well." She cleared her throat. "Did Ms. Corbin tell you why I'm in need of your services?"

"Just what you told her. Someone is trying to extort money from you."

"Yes. A lot of money."

"And you have no idea who it is."

"None. I can't imagine anyone who would do such a thing."

"How did this person contact you?"

"By telephone. Two calls so far, the first two nights ago, the second last night . . . in the middle of the night. The voice had a funny muffled sound, as if he was talking through some kind of . . . I don't know, a filter or something."

"You said 'he.' You're sure it was a man?"

"Well . . . no, not positive. I just had that impression."

"We'll leave it at that for now, then. What exactly did he say?"

"That he . . . had proof of something in my past that would put me in prison if he took it to the police. But that's just crazy. I've never done anything wrong in my life."

"Did he indicate what he thought you'd done?"

"No. He laughed when I told him he had no grounds for blackmail."

"So he wouldn't say the kind of alleged proof he had?"

"He wouldn't, no. Just that I'd find out when I paid him."

"How much is he demanding?"

"Five thousand dollars, the first time. Last

night . . . he said he changed his mind and he wanted double that amount. In small bills, nothing larger than a twenty."

A lot of money without any specifics to back up the demand. But extortionists were an unpredictable breed. "Did he say when or where he expects you to deliver the money?"

"No. He said he'd tell me next time he called. And I'd better pay him or else he'd make me sorry, very sorry."

"Did you threaten him with the police?"

"I . . . no. Should I have?"

"Sometimes it scares them off," Runyon said. "Have you been in touch with the police?"

"No. No, I haven't. He warned me not to."

"It's still your best option. Extortionists are as afraid of the law as their potential victims."

"But I'm *not* afraid of the law. I have nothing to hide."

"Then why not go to the police? They have resources that private agencies don't in cases like this. For one thing, they can arrange to monitor future calls, trace the man that way if you can get him to stay on the line long enough."

"Can't you do that?"

"Not through the phone company, no."

"But there are other things you can do to find out who he is?"

"Before we get into that, please answer my question. Why not the police?"

Verity Daniels fussed with her hair, nibbled some of the paint off her lower lip. "I . . . had a bad experience with them once. The authorities."

"What sort of bad experience?"

"Over an accident, a terrible accident. But it couldn't have anything to do with this. . . ."

"Tell me about it anyway."

"Must I? The memories . . . they're still painful."

"You can leave out any details that aren't relevant."

"Yes, all right. The accident happened to a man I was engaged to . . . Jason, Jason Avery. We were on a weekend camping trip in the Delta. He went for an early-morning walk while I was still sleeping, and . . . I don't know, something happened, he fell into the water. He must have panicked because he couldn't swim and he . . . drowned." Ms. Daniels shuddered. "I found him after I woke up. He was lying facedown in mud and tule grass. I dragged him out on shore and tried giving him mouth-to-mouth, but it was too late, he was already dead."

"When was this?"

"Two and a half years ago. Do you have to write everything down?"

"It's customary, yes. You have no objection?"

"No. No, of course not."

"I take it there were no witnesses? Other campers, fishermen?"

"No. We were alone. That's why the police . . . sheriff's people, I mean . . . at first they didn't believe it was an accident, that we'd had some sort of fight and I'd done something to Jason, hit him with something and then dragged him into the water. . . ." She shuddered again. "An awful time in my life. Awful."

"But you were finally absolved of any wrongdoing."

"Finally, yes. They had to leave me alone in the end because I told the truth and they couldn't prove otherwise. If you're thinking that's what this person on the phone was referring to, you're wrong. I had nothing to do with poor Jason's death."

"Were there any problems with members of his family?"

"Problems? I don't . . . you mean a relative who didn't believe what happened?"

"Yes."

"Oh, no, his people were very supportive."

"Do you know of any enemies you might have, Ms. Daniels? Someone with a grudge against you for any reason?"

"No. You think this man could be somebody I know?"

"It's possible. Is there anyone who might resent the fact that you inherited a large sum of money? Family members, acquaintances?"

"I don't have any family, now that my aunt is gone. Or new friends since I moved to San Francisco. I . . . don't make friends easily." Pause for some more lip nibbling. "There's Scott, I suppose, if he knows about it, but I don't think he's capable of a vicious thing like this."

"Who would Scott be?"

"My ex-husband."

"Last name?"

"Well . . . Ostrander. I took back my maiden name when we divorced five years ago."

"Where does he live? Work?"

"I don't know. I haven't seen or talked to him since the divorce. The last I heard he was still in Orinda. That's where we lived while we were married. After the divorce I moved to Martinez, where my job was. I worked for an insurance company there, but after the inheritance . . . well, there wasn't any need to keep the job and I'd always wanted to live here in the city."

"What does your ex-husband do for a living?"

"He was a landscape engineer. That's what he called himself, but it's just a glorified name for gardener."

"Was the divorce amicable?"

"No divorce is ever completely amicable, is it? But it wasn't bitter, either, not really. We were married for two years and we just didn't have a lot in common. I finally made up my mind to end it."

"No resentment on his part?"

"There didn't seem to be."

Runyon asked, "What about people you knew and worked with in Martinez? Anyone you didn't get along with?"

"I can't think of anyone, no."

"In Orinda while you lived there?"

"Well, Scott's sister. Grace never did like me." A curled lip indicated the feeling was mutual. "She could be a bitch sometimes, pardon my language, but I haven't seen or talked to her since the divorce, either."

"Any serious trouble between the two of you?"

"Not really. It was just that I couldn't do

26

anything right and Scott couldn't do anything wrong. She always took his side."

"What's her full name?"

"Grace Lyman. L-y-m-a-n. She's married to a doctor, or was then — a pee doctor." Ms. Daniels blinked and made a little embarrassed tittering sound. "Urologist, I mean. Sorry about that."

"Anyone else I should know about?"

"I can't think of anyone." Ms. Daniels shifted position in the chair. "You *are* going to help me, aren't you?"

"If you're certain that's how you want to proceed. A police investigation is still your best option."

"After what happened when Jason was killed, the way I was treated . . . no. There's my charity work to consider, too. Any kind of publicity might be harmful to my fundraising efforts."

"The authorities can be discreet."

"Can they? Not as discreet as you and your agency. You have a reputation for honesty and discretion, that's what the newspapers said. You're not trying to talk me out of hiring you, are you?"

"Just being frank. What is it you expect of us?"

The question seemed to puzzle her. "Find

out who's doing this awful thing to me. And why."

"And then what? Scare him off? Have him arrested?"

"Whatever you think is necessary. Just so he never bothers me again."

Reasonable enough. If Verity Daniels was being truthful about her past, it looked as though she was the victim of an extortion ploy rather than a blackmail attempt. The "proof of something in the past" and the veiled threats smacked of a come-on, the kind that would be followed by direct threats of bodily harm unless she met his demands. If that was the case and the perp wanted money badly enough, she was potentially in danger.

"One more thing, Ms. Daniels. For the record, you should know that in the investigation of extortion cases, we're bound by law to notify the proper authorities if we uncover evidence of a felony involving the victim, and to turn over any physical evidence that might come into our possession."

"That doesn't apply to me. I told you that."

Runyon opened his briefcase, took out the standard contract the agency used for individual clients. While she looked it over, he outlined their fees. No questions. She signed the contract with a flourish.

While she was writing a check to cover the retainer, she asked, "What if he calls again tonight?"

"If he does, try to stall him for at least eighteen hours. Tell him you need time to get the money, or use any other excuse you can think of."

"Why?"

"So I can make what might be a necessary arrangement. I'll explain when and if the time comes."

"Well . . . all right. But I should contact you right away and let you know, shouldn't I? Whenever he calls?"

"Yes." He gave her one of his business cards with agency, cell, and home numbers on it. "You should be able to reach me any time, day or night." He asked her for her contact info — phone numbers, e-mail address — and added the information to his notes. Then he said, "There's one thing I can do now, if the extortion calls come in on your landline."

"They do, yes. I can't imagine how he got the number."

"Do you own a pocket tape recorder?"

"Why would you ask — Oh! To record the next call?"

"That's right. It's not admissible as evidence in court, but any record of a blackmail attempt is to your benefit."

"I don't own one, no. I've never needed to use one."

"Not a problem." From his briefcase Runyon removed the spare Olympus digital voice recorder and the telephone recording interface he'd brought with him. "You can borrow this one."

"Well, you come prepared, don't you."

"As much as possible. Where's your phone?"

It was on a table next to an archway into a kitchen alcove. Runyon hooked the adapter to the phone and plugged the other end of the wire into the recorder, while she stood watching in a fascinated way. "This allows both ends of the conversation to be recorded," he said.

"And I don't have to do anything?"

"Just turn the recorder on — this switch here — when you know it's him. It's voice activated."

She nodded, staring at the recorder and the interface as if they were curious artifacts. Not much into technology, Ms. Daniels.

"One more thing," he said. "When he calls, threaten him with the police this time. See what kind of reaction you get. But don't carry it too far — be careful not to antagonize him."

"Oh, I'll be careful. I'm always on my guard these days." She tittered again. Nerves, probably.

Runyon asked if she had any more questions. She took her time thinking about it, but not as though she were searching her mind; he had the impression she was reluctant for him to leave. But he'd been there long enough. When she said, no, no questions, he got immediately to his feet.

At the door she gave him her hand, smiling. Let it remain clasped in his a little longer than he thought was necessary. "Thank you so much, Mr. Runyon. Or may I call you Jake?"

"If you like."

"You don't know how much I appreciate this, Jake. You make me feel safe for the first time since those calls started."

Runyon rode the elevator down with the image of her smile lingering in his mind. It hadn't been one of relief, nor had it been impersonal. Bright, like in a dental ad on TV. Bright eyes, too. A smile and a look that were almost flirtatious. And that in retrospect struck him as oddly secretive.

2

He heard nothing more from Verity Daniels that night or Wednesday morning. No surprise there. Part of an extortionist's MO was the silent squeeze: keep the victim dangling for a while, make them sweat. He wondered if the ploy was working on Ms. Daniels. She hadn't seemed to be doing much sweating during the forty-five minutes they'd spent together.

At the agency he gave Tamara a full rundown on the interview, tacking on his vague misgivings. She rubbed at red-flecked eyes with thumb and forefinger while she digested the report. She looked tired, a chronic condition lately: working too hard since the hellish events in early July that had forced Bill into his leave of absence, evidently not sleeping well. She'd been the beating heart of the agency ever since Runyon had signed on, a twenty-seven-year-old workaholic who usually thrived on the demands of the job. But the long hours, the pressure of running what was now a five-person operation after the hire of two part-time field men, and her concern for Bill's and Kerry's welfare, had taken a toll. He suspected she wasn't eating much, either; she was thinner than he'd ever seen her, her round cheeks hollowed, the usually warm brown color of her skin now like chocolate diluted by too much milk.

She needed to scale back some, hire a temp to help her with the office work, but it wasn't his place to say anything to her. He didn't have the same kind of rapport with her that Bill did, or a long enough history with her to feel comfortable in stepping beyond their employer-employee relation-ship. Ever since Colleen's death he'd found it difficult to relate to people on a personal level, even those he knew fairly well — even Bryn, now that she'd regained custody of her son Bobby. The best thing he could do for Tamara was to keep putting in long hours himself, lighten her load as much as he could. Quietly, without fuss or complaint.

At length she said, "So you think maybe Ms. Daniels wasn't being straight with you? Withholding information?"

"Hard to say exactly. Mostly it was the way she conducted herself — not quite the way you'd expect a worried shakedown victim to act."

"She sounded pretty upset on the phone."

"Misconception on my part, probably. Victims aren't always consistent in the way they act."

"Well, I'll do some checking into her background and what happened to her fiancé, see what turns up."

"One thing," Runyon said. "It might be a good idea to have a Q-Phone handy. Okay to call George Agonistes for one?"

Tamara's mouth quirked into a mock grimace. "Poormouth and Cheap Investigations," she said. "I hate doing business with that guy, even if he is an old friend of Bill's. Sometimes I think we'd be better off if we built up our own stock of spy and surveillance equipment."

Simple electronic devices, like phone interfaces and voice recorders, didn't cost much to keep on hand, but the more sophisticated items like Q-Phones ran four figures. The agency didn't handle the kind of debugging and industrial espionage cases Agonistes specialized in, seldom had need of high-tech electronics. Cheaper in the long run to sub-hire or rent from him when a situation called for his type of expertise.

Tamara knew that as well as he did; the

grumbling was part of her mood this morning. She said, "Okay, go ahead. But he better not try to overcharge us again."

Runyon made the call, got Agonistes himself on the line. As had been the case with their agency, Agonistes's operation had expanded in recent years; he ran it out of a SoMa loft now, had three or four employees, and spent most of his time devising new and more subtle ways to spy or help others spy on individuals and institutions. Runyon wouldn't have wanted to make his living that way, but then most of the time he didn't have to.

He drove over to SoMa to pick up the Q-Phone. Agonistes, a bent stick of a man with bushy hair like a fright wig, insisted on activating the preprogrammed SIM card for him even though it wasn't necessary. Just part of the service, he said, which meant he'd use it to try to pad the rental bill. All it took was a couple of short text messages from Runyon's cell to the Q-Phone to turn it into a spy tool.

The rest of the morning and part of the afternoon he spent on an employee background check for one of the dot-com outfits that had their offices within shouting distance of South Park. Routine and time-consuming, like most of the agency's investigations. He was on his way to keep an appointment on another matter when Tamara buzzed his cell.

"Ms. Daniels called a little while ago," she said.

"Heard from the perp?"

"Not yet. Call was about you — how professional you were, how relieved she was to have you helping her." Tamara added with wry humor, "Got yourself a big fan there, Jake."

Just what he needed. He remembered again that odd bright smile she'd given him at the door, the faintly flirtatious look. One of those attractions that every now and then a woman client developed for a helpful detective? Hadn't felt like that, exactly, but you couldn't always tell. He hoped that wasn't it. Even if it weren't for Bryn, he wouldn't have been interested. Verity Daniels could've been a *Vogue* model wearing a see-through negligee last night and he wouldn't be interested. Firm rule established during his cop days in Seattle: never get personally involved with anyone for any reason on the job.

He said noncommittally, "Yeah. Big fan."

"Well, she's not Ms. Sunshine. Got some truth issues, that's for sure."

"How so?"

"For one thing, her inheritance didn't come from an actress aunt who lived in Paris. Came from an uncle, her only living relative. He won one of those megabucks lotteries back east several years ago, then surprised everybody by keeping his job as a mechanic and investing most of the money. Died with about two million bucks in liquid assets. Could be she invented the aunt because a windfall from a rich and famous relative sounds way more cool than one from an ex-mechanic."

"What else?"

"Her marriage. She didn't divorce Scott Ostrander, he divorced her. And it was the messy kind. Hassles over community property and an alimony demand on her part."

"She get the alimony?"

"Nope. Judge wouldn't give it to her. Her salary at the time was almost as much as Ostrander was making in his landscape business."

Another face-saving lie, maybe. Hadn't wanted to make herself look bad. "What's Ostrander doing now?"

"Still in Orinda — owns a nursery, operates his landscaping service on the side. Remarried three years ago. No record, but he could still be the extortionist."

"Five years is a long time to hold a

grudge."

"Not for that reason," Tamara said. "Financial troubles. Running both his businesses in the red, behind on a bank loan and facing foreclosure. Damn economy again."

"Anything on his sister, Grace Lyman?"

"Nope. Still married to the urologist and living in Danville. No trouble with the law. And a perfect credit rating."

"The drowning accident? Straight story there?"

"Pretty much, except for two things. The county sheriff's people didn't hassle Ms. Daniels — just held her overnight as a material witness while they investigated. No witnesses, no marks on Jason Avery's body or other evidence of foul play, so they turned her loose and closed the books. Over protests from Avery's mother and brother — that's another lie she told you, about his family being supportive."

"They didn't believe it was an accident?"

"Weren't satisfied with the official verdict," Tamara said. "They stopped short of accusing her of murder, but they weren't convinced she was telling the whole truth about the drowning."

"Why not?"

"He was on the verge of calling off the

engagement. According to his mother, that was the reason he agreed to the camping trip — one last try at saving the relationship, and if that didn't work, end it then and there."

"Why was he thinking of calling it off?"

"All he'd say was that he felt he couldn't trust her anymore. That was what the mother told the sheriff's people, anyway. Maybe he found out she was getting it on with somebody else. Whatever the reason, the mother and Avery's brother figured he went ahead and dumped her, she freaked, there was some kind of confrontation, and he ended up dead in the water. Could've gone down that way."

Runyon asked, "Either the mother or brother need money?"

"Yep. Helen Avery's still recuperating from gastrointestinal surgery, has minimal medical insurance. Hank Avery lives with her, takes care of her. Divorced, works for an outfit in Walnut Creek that cleans and repairs roof gutters. Low-income job."

"How long ago was the mother's surgery?"

Pause while Tamara checked her notes. "Eight months. Complications put her back in the hospital once not long after."

"Verity Daniels collected her inheritance six months ago."

"Right. So if it's the Averys, how come they didn't try shaking her down then?"

"Maybe they didn't find out about it until recently."

"They'd still need some leverage, though, some reason to believe she'd pay ten K. Proof she offed Jason?"

"Not too likely after two and a half years."

"No, probably not."

"There's another flaw in that theory," Runyon said. "If she did have something to do with the drowning, why come to us? Why not just quietly pay off? She can afford it."

"Maybe she's more scared than smart."

"Not that scared and not stupid. Whatever's behind this, she's still a victim."

"And our client, despite the lies," Tamara said. "Better she should be paying us than some sleazeball extortionist."

3

Runyon stretched out his workday until six-thirty, then lingered over a solitary dinner at a Chinese restaurant in the Inner Sunset. He wasn't seeing Bryn much except on weekends now, and then only for a meal or a movie that included Bobby. Their relationship was winding down; he knew it and she knew it, though neither of them had brought it out into the open yet. They'd slept together exactly once in the past two months, a hurried coupling that hadn't been good for either of them because it lacked the hunger, the closeness, the tenderness they'd shared when they had no one but each other to cling to.

Thing was, she didn't need him anymore. From the first their connection had been based on loneliness and desperation — two damaged people, Bryn suffering the effects of the stroke that had crippled the left side of her face and the bitter divorce and custody battle that followed, him crippled by what had seemed then to be an unshakable grief. They'd reached out to each other, helped each other hold the demons at bay while they struggled for survival. Bryn had told him once that he'd literally saved her life: more than once before they met she'd edged close to suicide. And in turn she had given him the strength to come to terms with Colleen's death, to finally regain some balance in his life.

But now she had Bobby again — the center and focus of her existence. It was the boy, not Runyon, who had lifted her up out of the depths and restored her will to live. Still room for him in her life, but it was a narrowing space, the kind reserved for friends, occasional confidantes, pro forma lovers. As close as they'd been for a time, the closeness had never reached the level of love or long-term commitment — never could, never would. The shared sex had been another way to combat the loneliness and the hurt — gentle embraces in the dark that lacked a deeper emotional commitment.

He got along well with Bobby, knew the boy looked up to him, but friendship was as far as it went there, too. Bobby already had a father, even if Robert Darby was a piss-poor role model; Runyon had no desire to become a surrogate competitor; and the bitter divorce had soured Bryn on marriage. Maybe she'd change her mind if she met the right guy, but that wasn't likely to happen. Too self-conscious about her handicap, too busy with Bobby and her graphic design business, to get into the dating scene. Runyon had the sense that if she never formed another relationship, never slept with another man, it wouldn't matter a great deal to her. Her life as she'd restructured it would be acceptable enough even after Bobby reached manhood.

He wondered if the same went for his life. Maybe. He could live without a woman because he could live with himself again. He had his work; it was all he really needed. And yet his mind and his heart were open to more now, if the right opportunities presented themselves. Another woman, one he could relate to on a simpler, less emotional level. Another attempt at ending the estrangement with his son Joshua. A lifestyle change of one kind or other. Something positive, in any case.

Even though loneliness and grief no longer plagued him, he still resisted going home at night. Home: a four-room flat on Ortega, in the city's west-side fog belt. A

TV for noise, a stove to brew tea and cook an occasional meal, a bed to sleep in. When he'd first moved in, before meeting Bryn, it had seemed like a cage he shared with Colleen's ghost. The only difference between it and a prison cell was the fact that he had a key to the door. Oppressive to the point of claustrophobia sometimes. Not anymore. The stifling effect of bare walls and cheap furniture had ended along with the haunting. Now it was just a familiar place he occupied until it was time to go out into the world again.

There was no garage in his building; tonight he had to park around the corner on 17th Street. A strong wind off the Pacific forced him into a forward hunch on the walk to his building. He barely noticed. Weather conditions had mattered to Colleen — Seattle's chains of rainy days sometimes depressed her — but they made no impression on him unless they affected his work. Wet, dry, warm, cold, windy, foggy — you had to deal with all the variations at one time or another, so why pay attention when there were more important things to deal with?

A while back somebody had spray-painted what looked like gang symbols on the wall next to the building's front entrance. Graffiti was a big problem in the city, even out here in a neighborhood that was predominately Asian and had no serious gang activity. The landlord had whitewashed over the tags, but you could still see the outlines. A minor crime, property defacement, but it went against Runyon's grain just the same. No one had the right to intrude on others' lives for their own benefit or amusement.

Inside his flat, he turned the heat up to chase the evening chill and checked his answering machine. No messages. Seldom were except for telemarketing crap, but his home number was also on his business card. He was in a stay-connected business in a compulsively stay-connected society: you had to cover all the bases.

He booted up his laptop. Three new e-mails, none of any importance. All right. He kicked off his shoes, turned on the TV to one of the handful of channels that specialized in old movies, turned the sound down, tuned himself down, and sprawled out on the couch. The interior tuning down was a trick he'd first learned on police stakeouts, resorted to more and more as a defense mechanism over the months it took Colleen to die by degrees. The less you let yourself think, the less pain and helplessness you feel. That was the theory, anyway.

Now it had become a habit, the best way he knew to get through the downtime periods that separated work and sleep.

He was no longer paying attention to the Bette Davis film, letting the drone of voices put him into a half-doze, when his cell phone vibrated.

Immediately he was awake and alert, another trick he'd learned in Seattle. The time digits on the TV cable box read 9:18. He checked the window on the phone: no caller ID. Verity Daniels, he thought. Right.

"He just called again, Jake," she said. She sounded a little breathless, not so much upset as excited. But you couldn't always trust voice impressions on the phone. "I recorded the conversation like you told me to."

"Everything that was said?"

"Yes."

"Did you threaten him with the police?"

"He just laughed. He wants the money tomorrow. If I don't bring it to him, he said . . . he said he'd hurt me. Bad."

"Bring it where?"

"Baker Beach at noon."

"In what kind of container, did he say?"

"A beach bag."

"And then what?"

"Wait for him. That's all."

"Wait where exactly?"

"By the rocks at the north end," she said. Then she said, "The secluded part of the beach beyond is clothing optional . . . you can sunbathe there in the nude. Did you know that?"

Runyon ignored the question. "Is that where he wants you to wait, on that side?"

"No. By the HAZARDOUS SURF sign on the main section."

Extortionists were usually wary of meeting their victims in daylight hours in a public place. Their normal MO was a night drop somewhere private, nobody else around to witness the exchange. Baker Beach was liable to be moderately crowded at noon, given the good late September weather, which meant more risk on his part. Why, when he'd been careful to remain anonymous so far? Either he was none too bright, or he had what he considered a good reason for making such an arrangement.

"Jake . . . I should keep the rendezvous, shouldn't I?"

"Yes."

"With the money?"

"That's up to you. But if you bring at least a small amount and he takes possession, it constitutes proof of extortion."

"And you'll be there to arrest him?"

"Depends on the circumstances."

"What do you mean?"

Runyon said, "He may send somebody to get the money for him, to avoid showing himself to you. We'll talk more about that when we meet."

"Meet? You mean before noon tomorrow?"

"Yes. For a couple of reasons. There's a café on the Embarcadero near your place, the Bayside Java House, Pier Fourteen. I'll be there at nine o'clock."

"Does it have to be in the morning? Couldn't you come over tonight?"

"Not at this hour."

"It isn't that late." Pause. "I'm scared, Jake. Really scared."

Trying to make it personal again. He said, "The Bayside, nine o'clock. Good night, Ms. Daniels."

No response, just a sharp click in his ear.

She was no longer annoyed with him on Thursday morning, and she didn't seem particularly scared or anxious, either, when she came into the Bayside Java House. Smiling. Heavily made up. And not dressed for the beach yet, unless she was planning on keeping the date with her tormentor in an expensive summer dress and high heels. The outfit was for his benefit, he thought. She couldn't even keep a simple business meeting impersonal.

The café was crowded, not a good place for the kind of conversation they were about to have. He steered her to the counter, ordered containers of coffee to go, and when they were ready, led her outside and down the Embarcadero to a bench near one of a bunch of massive public art sculptures that the city fathers seemed to think had aesthetic merit. Her smile by then had given way to a puzzled frown.

It was in his mind to say something to her about the lies she'd told, ask her to explain herself, but he didn't do it. This wasn't the time or place. And unless it had something to do with the shakedown, her moral integrity was of no real importance anyhow.

He gave her the Q-Phone. The frown deepened as she turned it over in her hand. "I already have a cell phone."

"Not like this one. It operates like a regular cell, but it has a special program that lets me call the number and open the line without any ring or message on the display screen."

". . . I don't understand."

"It also has sensitive built-in microphones that'll pick up any sound within a reasonable distance. Designed for listening in on cell-phone conversations, short- or long-distance. But it works just as well for picking up face-to-face conversations when the line is open."

"Oh. Oh, I see. Even on a public beach?"

"Even there. I should be able to hear everything you and whoever makes the noon contact say to each other."

She turned the Q-Phone over in her hand, looking at it now as if she found it fascinating. "Is something like this legal? Not that I care if it isn't."

"Perfectly legal." Though there were some who felt that it shouldn't be. "If the contact is somebody you know, use his name. If it's a stranger, say something to tell me so."

"Then what will you do?"

"Depends on the circumstances. Leave that to me, Ms. Daniels."

"Verity. Please." Then, "You'll be very close by, won't you? On the beach?"

"Close by, yes, but don't look for me. You may be watched beforehand — don't do anything to call attention to yourself."

"I won't. What should I say to him?"

"Just follow his lead. And comment on the alleged evidence so I'll know what it is."

"He can't bring what doesn't exist."

Runyon said, "Chances are he'll have

something to show that he thinks is incriminating enough to buy him ten thousand dollars. Photos, documents real or faked . . . something tangible."

"Yes, I see what you mean."

"Try to get him to give it to you, whatever it is. If he refuses, don't insist. Agree with whatever he says and let him walk away with the money."

"In other words, don't make waves. Just let the ocean do that, right?"

Runyon ignored that. "Don't call me after the exchange," he said. "I'll be in touch as soon as I have something to report."

"Whatever you say, Jake. I'm completely in your hands."

She wanted to sit and talk while they finished their coffee; he didn't. Preparations to make, he said, ignored the hand plucking at his coat sleeve, and left her sitting there in a half-pout.

The meeting left him with the same off-kilter feeling he'd had after his previous encounters with her. She was scared, she'd said, but she seemed as eager to have him call her by her first name as she was to have him protect her. The nude sunbathing comment last night and the one today about the ocean waves . . . both inane and uncalled for, and both punctuated by a hint of girlish giggle.

She seemed reasonably intelligent, reasonably stable, but you couldn't always tell. A head case? Getting off giddily on the sharp edge of danger? Coming on to him for the same reason? He'd come in contact with a few of that type over the years, but Verity Daniels didn't display any of the usual, obvious symptoms.

He couldn't figure her out. And he had a feeling he wouldn't like her any better if and when he did.

4

Runyon had never been to Baker Beach. Driven past it any number of times on his restless roamings around the city, and because the road that ran past it, Lincoln Avenue, was the shortest route from Sea Cliff and other points on the far-west side to the Golden Gate Bridge. But there'd been no reason for him to set foot on the beach itself. He had no interest in scenic views, crowds of sunbathers, and families with kids and dogs. A couple of times he'd gone on picnics with Bryn and Bobby, but neither outing had been in the city. And Bryn was too self-conscious about the frozen side of her face, even covered by the scarf she always wore in public, to want to make a habit of it.

He knew a little about Baker Beach now because he'd Googled it last night after Verity Daniels's call; he'd always been leery of going into unfamiliar territory on an assignment without some idea of what it was like. The beach stretched along the foot of serpentine cliffs on the northwest shore, part of the Presidio that had once been military land and now belonged to the Golden Gate National Recreation Area. Mile long, broken up into two sections, the smaller one to the north allowing nudity because it was on federal land. Unsafe for swimming: large waves, riptides, and undertow. Original site of the Burning Man festival before it moved out into the Nevada desert in 1990. More data than he needed, but he'd filed it away just the same; you never knew when bits and pieces of background information might be useful.

He'd looked at a dozen or so posted photographs, too, to get a visual sense of the place, among them several of the HAZARDOUS SURF sign and the little rocky peninsula that separated the two parts of the beach. So he knew what to expect when he swung off Lincoln Drive a few minutes before ten on Thursday morning, turned onto the road that led to the north parking lot.

Last night's wind had died down to a mild breeze and the day was already starting to warm. The good weather had brought people out early; the parking lot was already a third full and some of the picnic tables scattered through the cypress grove flanking the road on the inland side had been claimed. Runyon wore casual clothes — Levi's, loose-fitting shirt, the only pair of shoes he owned that were appropriate for the beach. And he had the right props: a towel, a bottle of mineral water, and his Nikon camera strap-hung around his neck. His cell phone was in his shirt pocket.

What he wouldn't take with him was the .357 Magnum he kept locked in the glove compartment. For one thing, his carry permit didn't extend to federal land. But even if it had, he wouldn't have done it. You'd have to be an idiot to bring a loaded handgun onto a crowded public beach. Even a direct confrontation with the perp, if it was the perp who showed, would be foolish in a place like this. There were only two ways off the beach, this parking lot and the other one farther south; easy enough to follow his man when he left, no matter who he was, and brace him elsewhere.

Runyon parked near the entrance to Battery Chamberlin, the remains of a WWII gun emplacement. The path down to the beach ran alongside the battery fence; he made his way past another warning sign, this one telling you straight out that people had died swimming and wading here. The beach was fairly narrow, extending south in a gentle curve to where the backsides of expensive Sea Cliff homes stretched along the seaward bluffs. The Google sites had touted panoramic views — the looming towers of the Golden Gate Bridge, the long sweep of the Marin Headlands across the Gate — but they might as well have been props, too, for all the attention he paid to them. He wandered down toward the surf's edge, then angled over toward the HAZARD-OUS SURF sign to familiarize himself with the area first-hand.

Some place for a blackmail exchange, out in the open and with no easy exit. Maybe the perp had picked it for that reason, but still it seemed a curious choice. There were plenty of secluded or semi-secluded places in this general area that offered more privacy.

Runyon pretended to take photographs of the headlands, the bridge, the low sloping area of dunes and sea scrub that stretched from the beach back up to high cliffs and thick cypress forest. Then he backtracked past scattered groups of people to a spot next to a post-and-wire fence at the dunes' edge — closer to the exit into the parking lot than to the warning sign. He spread his towel there, sat down in the sun. His wait would be almost an hour, but that was all right. Waiting didn't bother him, and it was always better in a case like this to put yourself in position as early as possible. He sat with his thoughts cranked down but his senses alert, watching people come and go and stroll along the waterline, dogs playing in the surf and kids tossing Frisbees and footballs back and forth.

The beach began to fill up as noon approached. Runyon's scanning eye picked out and studied men and women who appeared to have come by themselves and who either sat or wandered near the north-side rocks. Pretty good bet that whoever showed up to collect the money would be by himself. Most of the beachgoers were in groups and pairs, but there were a few solos of both sexes. A fat woman in a sun hat perched Buddha-like on a towel not far from where he sat. A middle-aged man walking his leashed dog. A younger, red-haired man leaning against one of the rocks, watching the low-tide waves roll in. None of them seemed concerned with time or the HAZARDOUS SURF sign.

Runyon watched the redhead by the rocks. But he was just another beachgoer who soon tired of looking seaward, turned away, and walked back along the waterline to the south.

Verity Daniels arrived ten minutes early. Runyon glanced at his watch when he saw her come shuffling through the sand from the parking lot. Now she was dressed for the beach: bright yellow blouse, red shorts, red sandals, floppy red hat covering her dark hair and shading her eyes. Gaudy on purpose, he thought, to make sure he wouldn't miss spotting her. A folded towel was draped over one arm, and she carried an oversized red-and-white striped beach bag and a smaller straw handbag. The Q-Phone would be, or should be, in the handbag.

She passed within ten yards of where he was sitting. If she saw him, she gave no indication. Kept her head still and her gaze focused straight ahead. Following instructions, a point in her favor.

She walked directly to the HAZARDOUS SURF sign, spread out the towel without letting go of the bag, and sat down facing seaward with the bag in her lap. Runyon fiddled with his camera for a time, aimed it at the bridge spans while he adjusted the focus on the telephoto lens, then swung it down casually to where the client was sitting. The lens was powerful enough for him to make out the beauty mark above her chin. He'd have a clear view of whoever showed up to keep the appointment.

Except that nobody showed.

Noon came and went. Verity Daniels began to fidget as the time passed, shifting position on the towel, twice standing up for a minute or two, then sitting down again. Adults passed near her, some of them heading around the rocks to the clothing-optional section, but only one person stopped to speak to her. Runyon snapped up the camera; the lens showed him a buff blond guy in his twenties, wearing nothing but a bathing suit, grinning as he spoke to her and she answered, then not grinning anymore and turning away to disappear around the rocks. Abortive pick-up try. False alarm.

Twelve twenty.

Ms. Daniels still sat alone over there. Tension had begun to show in the way she moved, the looks she directed back along the beach.

Twelve thirty-five.

No-show for sure. Runyon knew it then, even if the client didn't. Both of them went on waiting, Runyon letting her dictate when they called it off.

It was almost one o'clock when Verity Daniels's patience ran out. She stood abruptly, snatched up the towel, and came fast-walking in his direction. Either she'd just seen him or spotted him earlier, because she was looking right at him. When she got close enough he shook his head once, jerked it once toward the parking lot. She hesitated, chewing on her lower lip, and then went on past.

He thought that in her agitated state, she might wait and try to talk to him in the lot — an unnecessary risk. No way to be sure she wasn't being watched.

He stayed where he was, letting more minutes tick by.

Thinking: dry run. Why?

"I don't know how much more of this I can stand," Ms. Daniels said. The words indicated she was badly upset, but her tone didn't give them any weight; it still carried that oddly secretive undercurrent. "All that time waiting on the beach . . . it was awful."

Runyon said, "Chances are he won't keep you on the hook much longer," because that was what she wanted to hear. "The money's too big a lure."

"Oh, I hope you're right. I don't feel safe anymore. I feel . . . well, violated. You know what I mean, Jake?"

"Yes."

"I never minded living alone, but now . . . just thinking about being by myself at night, waiting for the phone to ring, gives me goose bumps."

"You live in a secure building."

"I know, but I'm still alone."

"You could stay with a friend."

"I don't have any close friends, no one I'd want to share this nightmare with. I don't know who I can trust anymore. Whoever is doing this to me could be somebody I know."

Probably was. But he didn't say it.

"I don't even want to go home now, in broad daylight." She was in her car, breaking the law talking on a cellular while driving; he could hear traffic noises in the background. He was in his car, too, but the Ford was still parked in the lot at Baker Beach. "I'm just too upset. I need to talk to somebody . . . in person, I mean, someone I know I *can* trust. Could we meet somewhere, Jake? Would you mind?"

Clients who continually wanted their hands held were a potential liability. But maybe another face-to-face would let him get a better handle on the woman. He said, "Where are you now?"

"Just turning off Bay onto the Embarcadero. I could meet you at Gordon Biersch or

Delancey Street for lunch . . . I'm starving. Or would you rather come to the condo?"

"You have the recorder with you?"

"Recorder? Oh . . . no, I left it home."

"I'll meet you there, then. I should listen to the conversation you had last night."

"But . . . his voice was disguised."

"I still might be able to tell something from what was said. Man or woman, at least, from the words, phrasing, inflection."

"Yes, I see. All right. How long will you be?"

"Half an hour, maybe a little less."

"Good. Then I won't be alone for too long."

On his way across town he reported in to Tamara, using the hands-free device hooked to the dashboard so he could talk while driving. He didn't say much about his take on Verity Daniels's unconventional behavior. You didn't have to be completely comfortable with a client to do the job you were hired for.

"So why do you suppose the dude didn't show?"

"For all we know he did show," Runyon said. "Sat off watching same as me, but didn't make contact for reasons of his own."

"Afraid she might've gone to the cops to

set a trap for him?"

"That's one possibility. Another is that he's looking to put the squeeze on even tighter."

"Demand more than ten K next time?"

"Either that, or a shakedown's not his primary motive."

"No? What, then?"

"Campaign of terror. Payoff in fear, not necessarily cash."

"A revenge thing? I don't know, Jake. You want to terrorize somebody, seems to me there're more up-front ways to do it."

"Not if your aim is slow torture."

"Still. Couldn't expect to play it this way indefinitely."

"No, and that's the worry. It might not be enough to satisfy him."

"You mean he might go through with his threat to hurt her?"

"It's happened before."

"Oh, man . . . You think he'll make contact again soon?"

"Hard to tell. Sooner than later."

"Sooner the better," Tamara said. "I don't like these iffy cases."

Neither did Runyon.

The first thing Verity Daniels said to him when she let him in was, "You know, I saw you on the beach with your camera. Not at first, you told me not to look for you, but while I was waiting. I couldn't help looking around then."

There was nothing for him to say to that. He dipped his chin.

"It made me feel less apprehensive. Knowing you were close by, I mean."

Another dip.

"Would you like some lunch? I don't have much in the fridge, I usually go out to eat, but I can make us a sandwich. . . ."

"Thanks, but I can't stay long."

"Well, you have to eat —"

"Two meals a day, breakfast and dinner. I'll just listen to the recorder and be on my way."

". . . All right. Whatever you say."

He went to where she kept the phone, started to unhook the interface, paused when he saw that the connector was loose in the recorder socket. He pulled it all the way out, pressed the rewind button on the recorder. The tape didn't move. He pushed Play. Nothing.

Ms. Daniels said, "What's the matter?"

"The conversation didn't record."

"It didn't? But I turned the machine on. . . ."

"The adapter wasn't plugged all the way

in. Did you disconnect it for any reason?"

"No. I didn't touch it." She made a flustered gesture. "But . . . I was so rattled when I heard his voice that I almost knocked the phone off the table. The plug must have pulled out then. Oh, God, I'm so sorry."

Runyon looked at her for half a dozen beats without speaking. She met his gaze, gnawing on her lower lip in that little-girl way she had, her expression hangdog.

"Jake?" she said. "Is it really that important?"

It wasn't, no, except for one thing. In spite of the guileless eyes and apologetic look, he had the sense that her explanation was false, rehearsed — another lie.

She hadn't loosened the connector by accident. She'd done it on purpose.

Why? Why would she lie about something like that?

No rational reason he could think of. If she knew who the extortionist was, because he'd identified himself or because the voice hadn't been disguised and she'd recognized it, it made no sense that she'd lie to protect him. She wanted him caught; hiring professional help, cooperating on the beach stakeout, seemed to prove that. Not recording the conversation, lying about it . . . counterproductive, acting against her own best interests.

Runyon didn't call her on it. If he was right, she would only compound the fabrication by denying it. If he was wrong, accusing her would be a breach of professional ethics. He reconnected the telephone interface to the recorder, making certain it was plugged in tight, listened to another round of apologies, and left her to the sterile luxury of her new home.

He'd had difficult clients before, but never one whose actions and motives were as puzzling as this one. For the most part people in trouble followed a similar pattern; they told the truth because it was the best way out of whatever bind they were in, lied and withheld information only when it reflected badly on them — never when it might thwart the efforts of the detectives they'd hired in the first place. Verity Daniels didn't fit that pattern. It wasn't just the lie about the recorder, or even the other lies she'd told. It was the behavioral inconsistencies, the impression that she had some sort of hidden agenda.

She had him off balance, a position he'd never liked being in. He functioned best when he was in control, when he knew what to expect in a given situation. It made him even more determined to see this assignment through, put an end to it as quickly as possible.

5

On Thursday afternoon he had a couple of scheduled interviews on an insurance case that took him to the East Bay. The interviews were in Oakland and over with quickly; by three o'clock he was on Highway 24 heading through the Caldecott Tunnel into Contra Costa County.

First stop there: Orinda, the closest in a short string of affluent bedroom communities that stretched out east of the tunnel. Ostrander's Nursery and Landscaping Service.

The place wasn't far off the freeway, in a semirural area with views of rolling, wooded hills. Modest-sized, tree-shaded; ceramic pots and other containers of flowers, plants, young trees, ornamental grasses spread out around a greenhouse with a closed-in wing on one side. Only two vehicles were parked on a small gravel lot in front: a van and a pickup, both several years old, both with the Ostrander name in a leafy design on the doors. Hot afternoon over here, temperature in the high eighties — one reason for the fact that there were no customers.

A short distance from the lot, a slender brunette was using a spray hose to irrigate a display of small flowering plants. She turned the hose off as Runyon approached, turned on a tentative smile. Early thirties, attractive except for a network of fine lines radiating outward around her mouth and eyes — more lines than there should have been at her age.

"Hello. May I help you?"

"I'd like to see Scott Ostrander, if he's here."

"Yes, but he's about to go back out on a job. I'm Karen Ostrander. Is there something I can do for you?"

"Thanks, but I need to speak to your husband."

"What about?" Warily.

"A private matter."

"If you're from the bank . . ."

"No, it's nothing like that."

Relief flickered briefly in gray eyes. "Well, he's in the greenhouse. You won't keep him long?"

"Not long, no."

The interior of the greenhouse was much

cooler, moist, thick with the mingled scents of earth and growing things. A lean, sandy-haired man was loading buckets of ferns onto a wheeled cart. Dampened wood chips made up the central pathway and the ones that angled off it through the greenery, muffled Runyon's footsteps as he approached.

"Mr. Ostrander?"

The man jerked upright, blinking in the filtered light. No smile appeared on his sun-weathered features: Runyon's suit and tie put him on guard the same as they had his wife. "Oh . . . yeah, that's me. Help you?"

"I'd like to ask you a few questions, if you don't mind."

"Questions? What about? Nursery items, landscaping?"

"No, that's not why I'm here —"

"The loan payments again? Look, how many times do I have to tell you people we're trying the best we can —" He broke off because Runyon was holding up the leather case that contained the photostat of his license. Ostrander squinted at it, blinked again; the shape of his expression changed. He said in an anger-mixed-with-frustration voice, "Don't tell me the damn bank's hiring private detectives to hassle me now?"

"I don't work for banks, Mr. Ostrander.

70

Or collection agencies. The reason I'm here has to do with a routine matter concerning your ex-wife."

"My ex-wife? Verity?"

"That's right. Verity Daniels."

The expression on Ostrander's thin, mobile face changed again, turned cold, hard, bitter. "I don't have anything to say about that woman."

"How long has it been since you've seen her, spoken to her?"

"Not since the divorce. If I never see her again, it'll be too soon. Now if you'll excuse me, I have work to do."

Runyon said, "So then you don't know about her inheritance."

Ostrander had turned away, was bending to lift another bucket of ferns. The words froze him for a few seconds. When he straightened again he wore a puzzled frown. "What inheritance?"

"From her uncle in Ohio. Six months ago."

"I didn't even know she had an uncle."

"Wealthy man. Won a state lottery, invested the money, left everything to his niece."

"The hell. How much did she get?"

"A substantial sum."

"How much is substantial?"

"Two million dollars."

Another shift of expression: astonishment this time. Five-beat stare. Then, unexpectedly, Ostrander burst out laughing. Loud, booming laughter that echoed and reechoed in the confines of the greenhouse. Vitriolic, without a trace of humor.

"Scott?" Karen Ostrander had come inside, was standing on the path behind Runyon. "For heaven's sake, what's the matter?"

Ostrander choked off the laughter long enough to say, "Two million dollars. The bitch, that crazy bitch inherited two *million. . . .*" And he was off again, the laughter hiccupping out of him now.

Karen Ostrander hurried past Runyon, took hold of her husband's arm and shook him until he choked it off again. "Who?" she said then. "Who are you talking about?"

"My ex. Verity." He wiped his eyes with the back of one hand, looking now as if he wanted to cry.

"Oh, no."

"Oh, yes. Christ, two million dollars!"

"Of all people who don't deserve that kind of windfall —"

"You know the woman, Mrs. Ostrander?" Runyon asked her.

". . . No. Only what she did to Scott."

"And that was?"

"Made his life a living hell for two years, then tried to hold him up for alimony when he divorced her."

"How did she make your life a living hell, Mr. Ostrander?"

"Every goddamn way possible."

"Affairs?"

"She's a conniving, cheating bitch," Ostrander said. "Verity. My God, if ever anybody was ever misnamed!"

"Did you know the man she was engaged to two and a half years ago, Jason Avery?"

Ostrander wagged his head. Runyon couldn't tell if it meant, no, he hadn't known Avery, or if he was refusing to answer the question.

"Avery drowned in an accident in the Delta. Did you know about that?"

This time Ostrander's entire body shook, not unlike a dog shedding water. "Listen, mister, I'm not going to talk about her anymore. Not after what you just told me. Not today, not ever."

"You'd better go now," his wife said to Runyon.

"Two million dollars," Ostrander said. "Jesus Christ!"

Another burst of laughter followed Runyon out of the greenhouse, into the after-

73

noon heat. This one was different from the others, thickened by more emotion than bitter resentment. Despair was one, he thought. The other was hatred.

It was 4:30 when Runyon rolled into Martinez. Small city on the southern bank of the Carquinez Strait that had been different things in its hundred and fifty years: gold rush and shipping boomtown, railroad switching point, home of Shell Oil refineries, sprawling bedroom community for the less affluent than those who lived in Orinda, Lafayette, Danville. Somebody had once told him it was the birthplace of Joe DiMaggio, and he had no idea why that had stuck in his mind. He'd never been much of a baseball fan.

Two stops to make in Martinez. He picked Gateway Insurance, where Verity Daniels had worked before her inheritance, as the first of them. As early as it was, Hank Avery might not be home yet from his job and Runyon's preference, if possible, was for a joint meeting with Avery and his mother.

The Ford's GPS led him into Martinez's old-fashioned downtown. The offices of Gateway Insurance were on a side street near the Amtrak station — a small, cramped space cut into two sections by a windowed partition. Half a dozen desks were packed close together in the outer two-thirds, only two of them occupied, both by middle-aged women; the inner one-third, behind the partition, was a private office. A slender, flaxen-haired man in his forties stood in the open doorway talking to one of the women.

When Runyon walked in, the man's demeanor changed immediately. His posture shifted from a sideways lean to arrow straight and a hopeful smile with a lot of white teeth in it flashed on like a neon sign. The smile would have been more effective if it hadn't been surrounded by a lot of tired-looking flesh etched with stress lines and red-rimmed blue eyes. He moved briskly enough across the office and introduced himself: Vincent Canaday, Gateway's owner.

The professional smile stayed put until they were closeted in the private office. When Runyon produced his license photostat and explained the purpose of his visit, the smile faded into a ghost of itself. Mention of Verity Daniels's name seemed to make Canaday uncomfortable, wary.

"Is . . . Ms. Daniels in some sort of trouble?"

"Why do you ask that?"

"Well, a private detective . . . and all that money she inherited . . . I just assumed it.

Is she in trouble?"

"I can't comment on the reasons for my investigation. Let's just say it's a routine matter."

"What is it you want from me?"

"The answers to a few questions, that's all."

Canaday sat down behind his desk, shifted his shoulders, folded his hands on the blotter. "What do you want to know?" he asked, the cordiality a little strained now.

"How long has it been since you've seen her?"

"The day she quit, six months ago. Didn't even give notice, just came in and told us about the inheritance and quit cold. Not that I blame her for that. I would probably have done the same myself."

"No contact since then?"

"No. No reason for there to be."

Something in the man's voice made Runyon ask, "What can you tell me about your relationship with her?"

"Relationship? Oh, you mean here in the office. Well, I don't know what I can tell you, except that she was a competent employee during the time I've owned the business."

"How long is that?"

"Six years come October. I was sorry to

lose her, but of course delighted to hear of her windfall. I . . . hope it's made a significant difference in her life, wherever she's living now, whatever she's doing."

"Did you suppose it wouldn't?"

"No, of course not. It's just that . . . well, sudden wealth doesn't always change a person, does it? Their basic nature, I mean."

"Not always, no. What would you say her basic nature was?"

Canaday cleared his throat, glanced at a framed color photograph canted so that Runyon could see it was of a red-haired woman and a boy of about twelve; his lips tightened and he cleared his throat again. "She seemed rather . . . lackluster, if you know what I mean."

"Not exactly."

"Not much personality. Bland, immature." He seemed to savor the taste of the words in a bittersweet way; his mouth moved as if he were rolling them around on his tongue. "She wasn't interested in the things most of us are. You know, politics, the economy, the environment. All she ever talked about was movies and TV shows. She didn't have . . . didn't seem to have any hobbies or interests."

"Boyfriends?"

"Not that I know about," Canaday said.

"She never spoke about her private life. In my hearing, I mean."

"She have friends among your staff?"

"No. No, she kept very much to herself."

"But she got along with the other employees."

"Oh, yes, sure."

"No friction with any of your customers?"

"None. No, nothing like that."

"So you'd say she was a model employee."

"I suppose so, yes. Did her job, hardly ever took a sick day."

"Honest, dependable?"

"Absolutely." The word came out hard, as if pushed through a blockage. Canaday unclenched his hands, looked at his wristwatch. "I don't mean to be rude, Mr. Runyon, but I have an appointment at five-thirty and I really should be leaving soon. If you don't have any more questions . . ."

"Not unless you have anything to add."

"Nothing, no," Canaday said. "Nothing at all. I've told you everything I know about the woman."

No, he hadn't. Hiding something, covering up — man with a guilt complex. Runyon would've bet Canaday had had something going with Verity Daniels at one time or another, and that it hadn't had an amiable ending.

■ ■ ■ ■

The man who opened the door of the house in one of Martinez's older tracts wore a uniform shirt that had the words *Riteway Gutter Installers* over one pocket. He was short, squat, with a blocky face dominated by a thick black mustache that bracketed his mouth and small, deep-sunk eyes under bushy brows. The eyes narrowed to slits when he saw that Runyon was nobody he knew.

"Mr. Avery? Hank Avery?"

"So? If you're a salesman or a religious nut, you better just haul ass. Like the sign right there by the bell says, no solicitors."

"I'm not a solicitor." Runyon proved it with his ID.

Avery stared at the license. "A private eye? What you want here?"

"A few minutes of your and your mother's time."

"You don't get any of her time. She's not well, she's sleeping. I asked you how come you're here."

"Verity Daniels."

The name made Avery jerk a little, tightened his mouth. He said, "What the hell?" and came out quickly onto the porch, closing the door behind him as if he were afraid his mother might overhear. "What about her? You investigating her?"

"I'm not at liberty to say."

"Damn well should be, if you're not. She killed my brother two and a half years ago. You know about that?"

"I know your brother drowned. And that it was ruled an accident."

"Accident. Bullshit. She killed him, all right. Even if she didn't hold his head under the water, she killed him. He'd still be alive if he hadn't gone on that camping trip with her."

"I understand he was thinking of calling off the wedding."

"Damn right he was. Should never of had anything to do with her in the first place."

"Why was he backing out?"

"He wouldn't tell me or Ma. Said she wasn't what he thought she was. No shit. Screwing some other guy, probably. Jason, he was big on a woman being faithful."

"If she was involved with somebody else, any idea who it might have been?"

"No. Could've been anybody." Avery cracked thick-knobbed knuckles. "She do something to somebody else? That what this is all about? Man, I hope so because then maybe she'll finally get what's coming to her."

"And what would that be?"

"Jail time, a busted head, whatever hurts her the most."

"Do the hurting yourself, Mr. Avery? If you had the chance?"

"Don't think I didn't think about it after Jason died."

"And?"

"Ma talked me out of it. Didn't want to lose her only other son on account of that bitch."

"The last time you had any contact with Verity Daniels was when?"

"Not since Jason died. Not long enough."

"Know where she's living now?"

"No, and I don't give a crap. Unless she's dead or about to be, so I can go to her goddamn funeral and then spit on her grave."

"So you hadn't heard about her inheritance."

Blank stare. "Inheritance? What inheritance?"

"From a wealthy relative. Six months ago."

"Her? *Her?* How much?"

"Seven figures."

"Seven — ! Goddamn it!"

Runyon decided to open up a little, see what kind of reaction he'd get. "What would you say if I told you somebody is trying to take some of it away from her?"

"What would I say? Good! I hope they get every damn dime that belongs to her."

"Would you try it if you thought you could get away with it?"

"Me? Hell, no. I wouldn't want none of her money. Only thing of hers I'd want is her blood."

"Is that a threat, Mr. Avery?"

Avery said, "I don't make threats, man," and turned abruptly and stalked back inside the house.

The three interviews hadn't netted Runyon much in the way of specifics, or pointed to any of the individuals as the perp. Each man seemed to have plenty of cause to dislike, distrust, openly hate, even fear Verity Daniels; any of the three could be guilty of extortion, terrorism, or both. Or none of them.

One thing the interviews had accomplished: he had a slightly better handle on Ms. Daniels now. She was a woman who engendered strong emotions in other people, all or most of them negative, either by design or because of personality flaws. Nobody seemed to like her much — and maybe that was the primary reason why she lived such a solitary life. Two million dollars might be enough to buy you a new home, a new look, all the possessions you wanted, but it wasn't enough to buy you a brand-new persona.

6

Verity Daniels called at 7:50 that night, while Runyon was heating a can of soup for a late supper. But it wasn't the right kind of call. She'd heard nothing more from the perp. She was half frantic from all the waiting, she said, and needed to hear a friendly voice. He had so much experience with this kind of thing and she had none — how long did he think it would be?

After the long day in the East Bay, Runyon was in no mood for telephonic hand-holding. "No idea how long," he said shortly. "I know it's difficult for you, Ms. Daniels —"

"Verity."

"I know it's difficult for you, but you'll just have to hang in until he decides to contact you again."

"It could be days, couldn't it? Even a week or more?"

"Not likely he'll make you wait that long."

"But it's so hard. I feel so . . . vulnerable, here all by myself. If I didn't know you were there to help me, I don't know what I'd do."

He had nothing to say to that.

"I don't suppose . . . I mean, is there any chance we could get together somewhere for a drink? Tonight if you're not busy, or tomorrow —"

"No, that's not possible."

"Just one drink, just for a little while?"

"No, Ms. Daniels. It's agency policy not to socialize with clients."

"But it wouldn't really be socializing —"

"I'm sorry, no. I don't mean to be unsympathetic, but I'll have to ask you not to call again until you hear from the extortionist."

Short silence. Then, in a different voice, clipped, edged with anger, "Yes, all right, I understand. Good night, Jake." She broke the connection immediately, the sharp click like an exclamation point at the end of his name.

Coming on to him, and angry at the rebuff? Sounded like it. Why? So maybe she had developed the kind of infatuation lonely women sometimes did for men who offered them a professional helping hand. Common enough, though he'd never had to deal with it before. Another possibility: underneath that bland exterior she was a sexual aggressor. Anger was sometimes the reaction of a rejected predatory woman. And the facts and implications he'd gathered today supported the supposition.

But neither possibility explained why she'd lied about the recorder. She *had* lied; he was sure of it. He wondered if her claim that she didn't make friends easily had been a lie, too. And her apparent blandness and loneliness a front. For all he knew she had dozens of sexual partners and came on to every man who interested her, including the hired help.

Some package, Verity Daniels. Lackluster on the outside, a tangle of contradictions, neuroses, hidden facets on the inside. Trying to unravel that tangle was like trying to reach inside an unfamiliar machine, grab a handful of twisted-up wires, and sort them out blind.

She called again at 11:45 on Friday morning. But this time it was business.

"I just heard from him," she said in a voice that wobbled a little. "My God, you should have heard the names he called me. Awful, disgusting names."

"Why the abuse?"

Heavy breath, as if sucked in hard through her teeth. "The police . . . he thinks I went to the police. He said that's why he didn't meet me at Baker Beach, because he knew he'd be walking into a trap."

Runyon said, "He couldn't know I was there. Testing you, trying to scare you even more."

"Well, he succeeded. God!"

"What did you say to him?"

"I told him he was wrong, I didn't go to the police — I followed his instructions, went to the beach alone with the money. He called me more names. He said I'd better be telling the truth because if he found out I wasn't he'd . . . he'd kill me."

Not good. Might be an empty threat, part of the design to exert more pressure . . . if simple extortion was his game. Blackmailers as a breed were generally nonviolent, menacing words their only weapons. But if the perp was driven by some personal motive such as revenge, the threat could be genuine. Had to be taken seriously, in any event.

He asked, "Then what?"

"He demanded I bring him the money today. No police, no tricks . . . or else."

"Baker Beach again?"

"No. Lands End. I'm to wait at an overlook on the Coastal Trail a quarter mile from the Fort Miley parking lot, where you can see what's left of old wrecked steam-ships. Does that mean anything to you?"

"No, but there are maps. What time?"

"Five-thirty. He's being very careful this time, he said. If he doesn't meet me by five-thirty-five, I'm to walk along the trail to where stairs lead up to the Veterans Admin-istration Hospital and wait there."

Which meant the perp would be watching the overlook for any signs of police pres-ence, and if he wasn't satisfied, he'd either make the meet at the stairs or somewhere between. Probably the latter.

"This time he wants the money in a backpack," Ms. Daniels said. "I don't have a backpack, I'll have to go out and buy one. . . ."

"All right. Did the conversation get re-corded this time?"

"Um, no. No, it didn't. But it wasn't my fault."

Runyon waited.

"He didn't call on my home phone," she said. "He called my cell. Because the land-line might be bugged, he said. How he got that number, too . . . I don't know. How could he know so much about me?"

Take her at her word, there wasn't any-thing else he could do. He said flatly, "We'll find out when we catch him."

"So you *will* be there? At Lands End? I don't think I could go through with this if you weren't. . . ."

"I'll be there. Same instructions as before — don't look for me, don't pay any attention if you see me. And don't forget to take the Q-Phone with you."

"I won't." She drew another sighing breath. "Jake . . . about last night. I'm sorry I bothered you, really I am. It's just that I was feeling so nervous, so lonely. Am I forgiven?"

Forgiven. As if she were a penitent seeking absolution. Or a wannabe lover trying to mend fences.

He said in the same flat voice, "We'll talk later tonight. Try not to worry too much about tomorrow."

"I won't." Another of her nervous little giggles. "I'll be on my guard."

The parking lot adjacent to Fort Miley at the end of El Camino Del Mar was less than half full when Runyon arrived at twenty past four. He'd been there before, but only on a drive-through. Lands End ran from Point Lobos down near the Cliff House all the way along the shoreline to the Palace of the Legion of Honor and the Lincoln Park Golf Course — a lot of rugged, wooded acreage criss-crossed by walking paths and hiking trails. As with Baker Beach, he'd never had cause to wander the area on foot. The extra time was necessary to familiarize himself with the area and the designated drop point.

He parked at the outer end of the lot. This time he did take the Magnum with him, slipping it into its clamshell belt holster under his loose-fitting shirt. This was city land, there were fewer people around, and the terrain was rugged enough in places to make ambush a possibility. He wouldn't draw the weapon unless he had to, wouldn't use it unless it meant saving the client's life or his own. But he felt better having it close at hand.

With the Nikon slung around his neck, he made his way down a steep set of wood-and-packed-earth steps to the Coastal Trail below. The sea breeze was fairly light today, carrying the pungent smells of sea salt and cypress. The maps he'd looked at told him the shipwreck overlook was to his right, away from the Sutro Bath ruins that lay below Cliff House. He took his time, stopping now and then to pretend to take photos of the Golden Gate Bridge and the rocky sweep of the coastline. There were a fair number of people on the path, on foot, on bicycles, pushing baby strollers, but their number would thin out by five-thirty.

The shipwreck overlook was maybe a quarter-mile from the parking lot, beyond where the wide asphalt path roughened into packed earth. It was long and wide, made of concrete with a row of benches in the middle, bellying out so that you could stand at the edge and look more or less straight down to the rocky shoreline below. The trail was open on both sides. Opposite the overlook, a manmade retaining wall had been built to contain sliding rock off the steep cliff above; a low extension of the wall stretched out on one side for twenty or thirty yards.

The wall was the only place to set up a surveillance, unless he wanted to sit or stand on the overlook itself. Neither option appealed to him. Conspicuous if he lingered in the area. A moving surveillance was tricky, too, potentially dangerous, but he'd have no choice if this was where the perp intended to make contact.

Runyon walked out onto the overlook. While he was standing there, pretending to line up a photo, a couple of twentysomethings came wandering in from the trail and stood at the outer edge staring down. The girl, a chubby blonde as Nordic fair as her partner was Mediterranean dark, said, "I don't see anything down there. You see anything, Jerry?"

"No. Must be high tide."

"What difference does that make? The signboard says you're supposed to be able to see parts of old shipwrecks, engines and stern posts, whatever they are. From the *Frank* something and two other old ships —"

"*Frank Buck.* But only at low tide."

She ignored that, asked Runyon to look through his telephoto lens and tell her if *he* saw anything. He looked and shook his head. "Sorry, no."

"I told you, Carol," the boy said. "Only at low tide."

"Oh, screw low tide, I wanted to see the old wrecks."

"I'd rather screw a young wreck like you."

She seemed to find that clever and funny; she giggled, swatted Jerry on the arm, then nuzzled against him, and the two of them wandered off in the direction of Point Lobos.

Runyon went the other way. The trail narrowed and roughened, winding through stands of cypress and pine and ground cover dominated by weeds, ivy, blackberry tangles. There were a couple of places along it where the perp could wait to intercept the client, if that was what he was planning. Nothing for Runyon to do in that case except shadow her as closely as he could and trust the Q-Phone to tell if and when he should make his move.

The stairs that led up to the trail above, El Camino Del Mar, and the VA Hospital beyond that, were a quarter-mile or so from the shipwreck overlook. A sign posted there confirmed it. The stairs, steep and curving, were set back in a flat little grotto in the middle of a long dip in the rock-and-dirt path. Runyon climbed upward into a sharp right-hand turn thirty yards or so above the trail. From there, the path was hidden by trees and outcroppings. He went up through another switchback to see if the grotto was visible from a higher elevation. It wasn't.

Back down to the grotto. Bad place for a stationary surveillance here, too. The trail ran more or less straight and open past the inclines in both directions, and vegetation crowded in close to it on the seaward side. If Verity Daniels got this far, the perp could come for the meet from any of three directions. And again Runyon would have to stay on the move and let whatever he heard over the Q-Phone dictate his actions.

All right. He had the lay of the land now, literally. He went back past the shipwreck overlook — it was deserted now — and on to the one below the parking lot. After five by then; Ms. Daniels would be here pretty soon. He sat on the low concrete wall, playing with the Nikon while he watched the stairs and the dwindling number of walkers, joggers, and bicyclists that passed by. The perp could be any of them, or none of them. Already here or on his way to the overlook from any of several directions.

What bothered Runyon about the setup was that no matter where the contact took place, there was no quick and easy escape route. If the perp was so worried about a trap, why pick Lands End in the first place? Once he had the money he'd have to walk a long distance, climb a bunch of stairs, to get himself out of harm's way. Unless he had a bicycle, but that would only take him so far. Reckless? Stupid? Neither trait squared with all the preliminary caution.

Verity Daniels showed at five-ten. Wearing a light white jacket over a bright red sweater, the backpack she'd bought strapped over her shoulders. There was a flicker of recognition when she saw him as she came off the stairs, but then she immediately lowered her head. He shifted his gaze seaward until she passed.

Runyon let ten minutes pass before he

flipped his cell open, tapped out the Q-Phone number. At first he didn't hear anything. If she hadn't brought it with her . . . But she had. The muted cry of a gull, a child's shrill yell from somewhere nearby. So far so good.

At 5:25 he got up and made his way toward the shipwreck overlook. Most of the walkers were in pairs; the only man alone he encountered was elderly and had a small dog on a leash. One youngish guy wearing a Giants cap passed on a bicycle, heading in the same direction. Possible.

He had the cell phone to his ear as he walked, moving his mouth as though he were holding a conversation. Five-thirty, and there wasn't anything to hear. Or to see when he came in sight of the overlook. Ms. Daniels was standing hunched near the edge, the pack like a Quasimodo hump on her back — alone, nobody else in sight.

Runyon closed the cell, put it away in his shirt pocket as he neared the end of the low retaining wall on the inland side. He stopped there, sat down to go through more pretense with the camera — unscrew the telephoto, replace it with a different lens. She looked his way, then off in the other direction, hugging herself as the now-chilly sea breeze quickened.

Two more minutes ticked away. A lean, balding guy wearing a tank top and shorts appeared from the opposite direction, paused to peer at the overlook signboard. Runyon tensed . . . but then the man moved on without looking at the client, without looking at Runyon, either, as he passed by. Nobody else appeared on the trail.

Five thirty-five.

Verity Daniels glanced at her watch for the third or fourth time, stood poised for a few seconds, cast a quick look in his direction, then left the overlook and started away down the empty trail.

Runyon let her get out of sight before he followed, putting the cell to his ear again. Still nobody around as he moved into the narrowing section of the path. And nothing to hear from the Q-Phone except faint background sounds, the thrumming of the wind.

Halfway through the quarter-mile walk to the grotto stairs, a huffing middle-aged runner passed him heading west. No one approached from behind.

And no one made contact with Ms. Daniels.

Quarter to six when Runyon reached the grotto. She was standing there looking upward along the deserted stairs, kept her back turned to him as he went by. He walked on up and beyond the incline by seventy-five yards or so, to where he could see a distance along the trail in both directions. Stopped at that point and stood listening, waiting.

Five minutes limped away.

And five more.

Another jogger appeared from the west, a woman this time, hydrating from a water bottle as she ran. No voices came over the Q-Phone.

Six o'clock.

He moved then, back to the grotto. Hurrying now. Verity Daniels was still alone, sitting forlornly on the bottom step. Her head lifted, eyes widening, when he approached her; she made a helpless gesture. That was all, no other display of emotion. The cold wind had put blotchy streaks of red in her cheeks.

"He's not coming," Runyon said. "Go on back to your car. I'll follow."

"But why? *Why* didn't he come this time?"

"Quick, and don't look back. I'll call you later."

She went. He gave her thirty yards and then followed, keeping her in sight all the way up to the parking lot and into her car. As far as he could tell, none of the handful of people still in the area paid any attention to either of them.

In his Ford he locked the Magnum away in the glove compartment, then sat for a minute or two with his hands tight around the steering wheel. Two straight no-shows. That had to mean the extortion demand was either a by-product or a smoke screen. Blackmailers by nature weren't timid, didn't bother with extended dry runs; they were in it for fast money, eager to get their hands on it, and ten thousand dollars was a lot of green. Persecution must be the perp's real intent. Slow, insidious, the threats of bodily harm possibly genuine. If he hated Verity Daniels enough, it wouldn't be much of a step from psychological torture to the physical kind.

And yet it still didn't feel right. His head said it did, his gut instinct said otherwise.

But if it wasn't extortion, it had to be terrorism, didn't it? What the hell else was there?

7

He spoke to Verity Daniels that evening, briefly. The second no-show had her upset, but not as upset as she should have been; there was that funny undercurrent in her voice again. He had no answers for her new round of questions and concerns, even less inclination than before to indulge her clingy need for reassurance, so he kept the conversation short. Truth was, her attitude and her penchant for fabrication had begun to erode the compassion he normally felt for crime victims. A client was a client, a job was a job, but even a man as committed as he was had his limits.

The uncertainty of what he was up against made the job that much harder, that much more frustrating. You couldn't identify the owner of a telephone voice you'd never heard, couldn't put the arm on somebody who refused to come out into the open. All you could do was wait for whatever happened next.

He drove to South Park on Saturday morning, as he sometimes did when he wasn't otherwise occupied, and Tamara was there as usual, talking to Bill on the phone. She gestured to Runyon to get on the line in Bill's office for a conference call. He did that, asked after Kerry. "Getting better," Bill said. "We're taking it one day at a time." He seemed in good spirits, upbeat, but Runyon couldn't help wondering if he were putting on a front so they wouldn't worry. Be just like the man to do that — think of the feelings of others in the midst of his own crisis.

It was Tamara who brought up the Daniels case. Evidently she'd been discussing it with Bill. Runyon had given her full reports on his East Bay interviews, the Lands End bust, his growing reservations, and she'd shared the information with Bill to get his input.

"If you're ready to dump it now, Jake, that's okay with us."

"You mean turn it over to Alex or Deron?"

"No, I mean dump it, period. Let her go to some other outfit. We've got a near-full caseload — we don't need any more of her money. Or any more of her lies. I caught her in another one yesterday."

"Oh?"

"Did some more checking on her," Tamara said. "All that stuff she fed us about fundraising for charities? Pure crap. Lighthouse for the Blind never heard of her. Nor has the Foundation for AIDS Research, or the Breast Cancer Fund, or any other charity organization I checked with. All fabricated so she'll look like a better person than she is."

"Insecure," Bill said. "And immature. People who tell the kinds of lies she does usually are."

"Screwed up, in any case."

Runyon asked, "Any indication of what she does do with her time?"

"Not that I could find out," Tamara said. "Doesn't travel — no record of airline ticket purchases or a passport application. Doesn't run up large credit card bills. Doesn't belong to Facebook or Twitter or Linked-In. Doesn't seem to do much of anything except sit on what's left of that money she inherited like a goose on a bunch of golden eggs."

Bill said, "Maybe she hasn't figured out what to do with it yet."

"*I'd* know what to do with it, that's for damn sure. Most people would."

"Most people have interests, hobbies,

101

goals. Jake's reports indicate she's one of the few who doesn't. No social life, doesn't do much except live vicariously through the idiot box."

"Then why move to the city, buy into a place like Bayfront Towers?"

Runyon said, "Told me she'd always dreamed of living in San Francisco. Her only dream, maybe."

"She had at least a couple of men in her life before," Tamara said. "You'd think there'd be plenty now, with all the green she's got."

"New in the city, hasn't met anybody yet who appeals to her." Except me, Runyon thought but didn't say.

"But she doesn't seem to be out looking. How come?"

"Her marriage was a bitter failure," Bill said. "Her fiancé was about to call things off when he died. Maybe the combination turned her off relationships."

"Not enough so that she wasn't screwing her boss."

"Jake's impression, not a proven fact. She could still be off men except for the occasional fling."

"Well, she's a liar for sure. And a pain in the ass. Looks to me like she's been both all her life."

"She's still in trouble," Runyon said.

"You positive about that? I mean, she's told so many other lies, maybe she's lying about the extortion, too."

"Why would she do that? What would she have to gain?"

"Who knows what goes on inside the head of somebody like her?" Tamara said. "But okay, give her the benefit of the doubt. She's in trouble, but it doesn't have to be our trouble anymore. Let her deal with it herself."

"Not a good idea. She talks a good fight, keeps saying over and over in a giggly little voice that she's on her guard. But that doesn't make her any less vulnerable."

"Hire somebody else, then."

"And start over from scratch."

Bill said, "It's your case, Jake. You want to stay on it?"

The smart answer was probably no, but Runyon's stubborn sense of commitment kept him from saying it. If he tried to put his feelings into words, Tamara might not understand but Bill would. They were alike in that respect. Seen too much human suffering to quit a case cold while the client was still in harm's way.

"Yes," he said. "At least until the perp makes his next move."

■ ■ ■ ■

Saturday passed without any more com-
munication from Verity Daniels. On Sunday
Runyon drove Bryn and Bobby down to the
Beach Boardwalk in Santa Cruz, a trip that
had been planned for a while but that he
almost canceled. Personal and professional
conflict: he ought to keep himself available
in case the client needed him, yet he also
had a right to some time off. He settled the
matter by calling Ms. Daniels, telling her he
would be out of town for the day and suggesting she turn off both her phones until
late evening. If the perp called and left her
a message, she could get in touch with him
any time after eight that evening. She
agreed, but he could tell from her voice that
she was reluctant, even a little annoyed.

The first half of the day was pretty good.
Bobby was excited — he'd never been to
Santa Cruz before — and he chattered all
the way down. The boy had opened up
considerably since moving back in with
Bryn; before that, because of the wrenching
divorce and the abuse he'd suffered at the
hands of his father's live-in girlfriend, he'd
been introverted, closed off. Good to see
him happy, acting and interacting the way

Runyon figured near ten-year-olds ought to. Bobby's enthusiasm was infectious. Bryn was more animated than usual, spent almost as much time communicating with Runyon as with her son.

The Boardwalk and beach were crowded and noisy. Warm day, plenty of sun, adults and kids trying to squeeze a little more merriment out of the fading summer. The three of them stayed off the beach — too jammed, for one thing, and Bryn was uncomfortable enough as it was wandering along the boardwalk. She wore a big, wide-brimmed straw hat pulled down low on the left side, so that it shaded the scarf-covered side of her face. But inevitably a few people stared at her anyway, openly wondering; a couple of callous teenagers smirked and pointed as they passed. Enough to dampen her spirits, focus most of her attention on Bobby.

The kid had a good time. Hot dogs, sodas, ice cream. Designing a T-shirt for himself in a shop that specialized in that kind of thing. Rides through the Haunted Castle below the boardwalk, on a 1911 hand-carved Looff carousel, twice on the Giant Dipper roller coaster, the second time with Runyon for company — Bryn refused to go. She wouldn't let Bobby go on something called the Double Shot, a 125-foot-high tower that shot riders up to the top and then back down again at the same speed so they could experience the weightlessness of negative-G forces. Too dangerous, she said. Scared her just watching the way it operated.

Runyon enjoyed the time with Bobby in an avuncular kind of way, but it left him with a lingering wistfulness, a rekindled sense of loss. If it hadn't been for Andrea, her alcoholism, her poisonous vindictiveness, he might have had outings like this with his own son while Joshua was growing up. Carnivals, ball games, barbecues, all the father-son closeness that she'd denied him . . . no, denied them both. Instead he and Joshua stood on opposite sides of the unbridgeable gap she'd created, strangers, the son hating the father because that was what he'd been taught to do. Andrea had died thinking she'd won, but there were no winners here. Only losers.

Bobby, tired out, napped in the backseat on the drive home. Bryn sat quietly against the passenger door, saying little. The fits of deep depression were a thing of the past, or so she claimed, but she could still be moody on occasion. Easy enough to figure why tonight: the boardwalk crowds, the few rudely staring and smirking faces, an awareness of handicap-induced alienation from normal activities such as swimming and sunbathing. At down times like this, when she was still living alone, she would have turned to Runyon for support, or responded to his offer of it, and they'd have talked her through it. Now, even though he tried, she said only, "I don't want to discuss it, Jake," and lapsed back into a melancholy silence.

She didn't invite him in when they got back to her brown-shingled house in the Outer Sunset. "I'm tired, Bobby's tired," she said. "A good day, but a long one. You don't mind?"

"No," he said, "I don't mind."

Bobby's hug was longer, more affectionate than Bryn's, his parting smile brighter. Quick brush of her lips over his, and she and the boy went inside arm in arm. Bobby looked back and waved before the door closed. Bryn didn't.

Winding down, all right. Like the summer. He felt it even more strongly as he drove home. From now on they'd be friends, because of the closeness they'd shared and because Bobby was his friend, but that was all they'd be. It made him a little sad, but not too much. Never any real doubt that the affair's end would come sooner or later, even though there'd been a time when he tried to convince himself otherwise — he saw that clearly now. In the long run Bryn, the handicapped Bryn, was better off alone. And so was he.

There were no messages on his answering machine. And he'd had no calls on his cell all day. He sat up until eleven-thirty, half watching a movie and then the news. Neither phone rang during that time, either.

Monday was another Verity Daniels–free day. Until 8:15 that night, when the damn case went crazy on him.

He spent the day wrapping up an insurance fraud investigation, then consulting with an attorney representing the wife of a deadbeat dad who'd skipped town owing five figures in child support. Dinner at another Chinese restaurant, not so much because he liked Mandarin and Hunan food as because it had been Colleen's favorite and eating it always brought back some of the pleasant memories of their twenty years together. Home to finish out the rest of his evening routine: blanking out in front of the TV until it was time for bed. Or so he thought until his cell vibrated.

As soon as he opened the line, before he had a chance to say anything, she made a half-grunting, half-crying sound, loud in his ear, and followed it with a rush of strung-together words. "God Jake oh God he was here he had a knife I thought he was going to kill me!"

"Slow down, you're not making sense."

Drawn breath like a steam hiss. Then, more coherently, "It was *him* . . . the black-mailer. Here. Right *here.*"

"In your studio?"

"Not at first, no, in the hallway. He . . . the things he said . . . and that knife against my throat . . ."

"Are you hurt?"

"No. But he scared me so much I'm still shaking."

"Did you notify the police?"

"The police? No. I don't trust the police, I told you that. You're the only one I trust."

"Building security?"

"No, it was too late by the time . . ." Gulping sound. "Jake . . . can you come over here? Now? It's not too much to ask, is it? I'll tell you everything that happened when you get here. Please?"

He sat for half a dozen beats, holding the cell tight in his fingers, before he said, "All right. Half an hour."

8

The same burly security man who'd been on duty the evening of Runyon's first visit was behind the desk in the lobby. The name *George* was stitched above the pocket of his uniform jacket. "Mr. Runyon, right," he said. "Ms. Daniels is expecting you."

"She say anything else when she called down?"

"Like what?"

"Like anything."

"No. Just that you'd be here about now."

"How did she sound?"

"Sound?"

"Upset, anxious, nervous?"

George looked puzzled. "Like she always sounds."

"Calm, then. Normal."

"That's right."

"Did you see her when she came back from dinner?"

"Tonight? No, sir. If she went out, it

must've been through the garage."

"The guard down there, Frank, said he hasn't seen her."

"Well, then, she must've been in all evening."

Runyon said, "Tell me something. How tight is the security in this building?"

"Why do you want to know?"

"Just curious. I'm in the security business myself."

"That so? What kind?"

Runyon told him, showed his ID. George frowned as he studied it. "Ms. Daniels didn't say anything about you being a PI," he said. "She in some kind of trouble?"

"Confidential matter."

George seemed to want to press him, settled instead for saying, "Sure, none of my business. I was a cop myself for four years, back in the nineties." He sounded bitter rather than proud of the fact. "Didn't work out, so I went into private security. Pays the bills, but it's not exactly exciting work. Not in a place like this."

"So the security's pretty tight."

"Tight as it gets. Nobody gets in or out unless they live here or they're invited or announced."

"Cameras on every floor? All working, all monitored by you?"

"On my shift, that's right."

"And you've been here all evening."

"Since I came on at four." One corner of George's mouth turned up in a crooked half smile. "Rules here are so strict I have to make an appointment to take a leak."

Verity Daniels opened the door so quickly after Runyon pressed the bell that she might have been waiting next to it. Maybe she had been. As soon as he was inside the studio with the door shut, she stepped in close and tried to embrace him, murmuring something he didn't pay attention to. He caught hold of her, not roughly but not gently, either, and stood her off at arms' length.

She blinked, looking hurt, uncertain. "I'm sorry, I didn't mean . . . I'm just so glad you're here. . . ."

"Tell me what happened."

"Can't we sit down first? I'm still shaky. . . ."

He let go of her, watched her walk to the blond-wood sofa and lower herself. When she saw that he hadn't moved, she said, "Aren't you going to sit down?"

"No. Tell me what happened."

"I went out to get something to eat . . . a restaurant just around the corner. I wasn't gone more than an hour. He . . . he was waiting when I got off the elevator. I didn't know he was there until he grabbed me from behind, told me not to scream or he'd . . . he'd cut my throat. I don't know where he came from, how he got into the building . . . he was just there, waiting for me. . . ."

She paused, looking up at Runyon in a beseeching way. He said, "You get a clear look at him?"

"No, he was wearing . . . you know, one of those ski masks."

"Recognize his voice?"

"No. Gruff, deep . . . I don't know. I was so scared. . . ."

"Then what?"

"He made me let him in and show him where I kept the money, the ten thousand dollars . . . it was still in the backpack. He said he didn't come for it at Lands End because he still didn't trust me. He . . . he made me lie facedown on the floor and threw a blanket over me. The last thing he said before he went away was that I'd be hearing from him again. He wants more money, Jake . . . another ten thousand. If I don't get it for him, he said . . . he said he'd come back again and *kill* me for sure."

Usually Runyon was slow to anger; it took a lot of situational pressure to build up heat, tighten his insides. Hot and tight now: it was an effort to maintain a blank-faced calm.

"Jake? What's the matter?"

He said, "The Q-Phone. Where is it?"

"In my purse. Why?"

"Get it for me."

She hesitated, then stood and went to where her purse lay on the breakfast counter that separated the living room from the kitchenette. She found the Q-Phone, gave it to him. He shoved it into his coat pocket, and without looking at her, crossed to the table where the landline phone sat. The interface was still hooked to it and the Olympus recorder; he disconnected the wires, put both items into the same pocket with the Q-Phone.

"What *is* it, Jake? Why did you do that?"

"I'm finished here, that's why."

"What do you mean? I don't under-stand. . . ."

"I'm not working for you anymore. Business terminated, as of now."

"Terminated? But you . . . you can't just walk out on me after what happened here tonight. . . ."

"Nothing happened here tonight."

"I was almost killed!"

"No, you weren't," Runyon said. "Nobody grabbed you in the hallway, nobody put a knife to your throat, nobody came in here and took money from you."

"How can you say that? He did, he did!"

"There's no way an outsider could get into this building with the security as tight as it is."

"Well, maybe he lives here!"

"That won't wash, either. Nobody who can afford to live in a place like this needs ten thousand dollars badly enough to run an extortion scam, or would risk picking a victim on his own turf if he did."

Sputtering noise in her throat. Violent headshake.

Runyon said, "Security cameras on every floor. If you'd been grabbed in the hallway, the cameras would've recorded it and the guards would have been up here in two minutes."

"He must have done something to the one on this floor —"

"Working just fine. George on the desk downstairs would've noticed if it hadn't been, sent somebody up to see why."

"Damn you, Jake! Why won't you believe I was attacked!"

"There's not a mark on you. Clothing's not disarrayed, makeup's perfect, not a hair out of place."

"I told you, he didn't cut me, he just

threatened to. I showered, changed my clothes, combed my hair —"

"All of that even though you were so scared you couldn't stop shaking? No, lady. Somebody holds a sharp knife pressed to your throat for any length of time, there's bound to be nicks, scratches, you couldn't wash away. Your throat is smooth. Get grabbed, held, muscled from behind, then thrown down on the floor, you'd have bruises, carpet scrapes. None of those anywhere on you, either."

The frightened-victim façade had begun to crumble. The shape of her mouth shifted, the crimson-painted lips thinning and pulling in against her teeth. Body rigid, hands opening and closing at her sides. Eyes darker, shinier, fixed on him in an unblinking stare.

Runyon, prodded by the slow simmer of his anger, kept hammering at her. "If I searched this place, I'd find the backpack was still here, wouldn't I? Empty, and not because the phantom intruder stuffed the cash into his pockets. There never was any payoff money. No home invasion. No threatening phone calls. No extortionist. It was all a hoax, wasn't it? One long string of lies from the beginning."

"No!"

116

"Why? Why play that kind of sick game?"

"I'm not sick! Don't you say that to me!"

"Your idea of a practical joke? Excitement, cheap thrills? Or do you just like messing with other people's lives?"

"No, no, no, no!"

"How long did you think you could keep it up? Long enough to get me into bed? Part of the fun, right?"

"Bastard!" The victim's pose was completely gone now. So were all the softer feminine qualities, real or faked. What was left was a kind of naked graven image: cold, feral, egomaniacal. "You can't just walk out on me!"

"Yes I can. You're worse than a liar, you're a manipulative cheat, and I don't work for cheats — my boss doesn't work for cheats. I resent the hell out of having my time wasted for your private amusement."

"I paid you for your time, I *paid* you!"

"Not nearly enough. Good-bye, Ms. Daniels."

He got halfway to the door before she came flying across the room at him. The move was sudden, as if she'd been launched off the couch; he saw her out of the corner of his eye, coming at an angle behind him from the left, and pivoted to set himself — not quite in time to get his crossed arms all the way up in front of his face. Her fingers were hooked into talons, the bright red tips glistening like daubs of blood. One of them snaked through his guard, slashed a painful furrow across his neck up under the chin, before he caught hold of her wrists, twisted her body sideways against the thrust of his hip.

She swiveled her head, still struggling violently, and spat in his face.

He held onto her just long enough to get leverage, then shoved her away from him. It was the only thing he could do short of subduing her with judo, possibly hurting her in the process. It wasn't a hard shove, but she stumbled anyway, lost her balance, went down on her ass on the carpet. The hem of her skirt bunched up over chubby thighs; she made no effort to pull it down. She sat there trembling, her eyes fire-black with hate.

"You son of a bitch!" she yelled at him. "You *cock-sucker*!"

Runyon wiped her spittle off his cheek, opened the door without turning his back to her, and got the hell out of there.

Driving across the city, the deep scratch under his chin burning like fire, he kept berating himself. He'd always considered

Jake Runyon to be nobody's fool. Well, for the past week he'd been somebody's. Fool with a capital *F*.

All the years he'd been a cop and a private investigator, all the cases he'd handled and people he'd dealt with on both sides of the law, all the fine-honed and usually reliable instincts, and still he hadn't seen all the way through Verity Daniels until tonight. Never encountered anyone like her before, but that was no excuse. Should have been alert to the possibility of deception, trickery; should have paid closer attention to Tamara's reservations and his own. Should have tumbled to the truth before tonight. All that slop about not trusting the police. The secretiveness, the inconsistent behavior, the flirtatiousness and inappropriate comments. The two straight no-shows at Baker Beach and Lands End. And yet his usually reliable shit detector had kept right on malfunctioning.

Too soft-hearted, too concerned with the client's welfare . . . No, that wasn't right. The client's welfare always came first, in any investigation. Had to: that simple rule was what the business was built on. If he didn't believe in it and follow it, he might as well go into another line of work.

His fault in this case, not the policy's.

He'd misjudged Verity Daniels, mishandled her and the situation — a mistake, an unprofessional error. Well, all right. Everybody makes mistakes. Learn from it, put it behind him, move on.

The strident buzzing of the doorbell sat him up in bed, instantly alert. The digital clock next to Colleen's picture on the bedside table gave the time as 12:51.

He'd been asleep less than two hours.

The bell went off twice more, insistently, while he threw on a robe, turned on a light, and padded barefoot across the front room. He said into the intercom, "Who is it?"

"Jake Runyon?" Male voice, unfamiliar.

"That's right."

"Police, Mr. Runyon. Mind letting us in?"

The skin pulled tight across his shoulders. Police showing up at this time of night meant bad news, nothing less. He thumbed the button that released the downstairs door lock, then belted his robe and opened the apartment door to wait.

They came up quietly enough, two of them, both in plain clothes. One Caucasian, heavy-set, in his fifties; the other Hispanic, younger, whippet-lean. He'd never seen either man before. They had their badges out, held them up for inspection when they reached the landing. Detective inspectors. Whitehead and Rodriguez.

Runyon stepped aside to let them in. They stood looking at him in silence, then around the room and at the open door to the bedroom. "Anybody else here with you, Mr. Runyon?" Whitehead asked.

"No. What is it you want?"

Rodriguez said, "We've had a complaint against you." Controlled aggression in his voice. The confrontational type.

"What kind of complaint?"

"You ought to know."

"But I don't. What kind of complaint?"

"Assault with intent to commit rape."

The anger began to bubble in Runyon again. He didn't say anything.

Whitehead said, "Aren't you going to ask who made the complaint?"

"Verity Daniels, I suppose."

"Well?"

"Did she tell you who I am, what I was hired to do for her?"

"She told us. She also told us you've been coming on to her the whole time, wouldn't take no for an answer. Called her up tonight, told her you had to see her on business. Became aggressive when she said no again, called her a bunch of nasty names and tried to attack her."

"None of that is the truth."

"You deny you were in her home earlier tonight?"

"No, I was there. She asked me to come."

"Why?"

No benefit in trying to explain the hoax. Take too long, and whether they believed him or not, it had no immediate bearing on the assault complaint. He said, "I'd rather not answer that right now."

"You deny grabbing her, trying to tear her dress off?"

"It never happened."

"Then how'd you get that gouge on your neck there?"

"Not the way she claims I did."

"That doesn't answer my question."

"Are you going to arrest me?"

Rodriguez made the kind of derisive noise young cops make when they think they've got a perp cold. Whitehead rubbed his hands together, hunched and rippled his shoulders as if he were cold.

"Let me guess," Rodriguez said. "You're not going to say anything else until you talk to your lawyer."

"If I'm under arrest, that's right."

Whitehead said, "Read the man his rights while he gets dressed, Benny, and let's get moving. It's cold as a witch's tit in here."

9

Booked, printed, allowed his one phone call, given an orange jail jumpsuit in exchange for his clothing and possessions, and locked away in a classification holding cell. Where he stayed. That was all right; he was better off alone, than if he'd been classified and maybe stuffed in with the night's roundup of violent offenders. The dangerous mood he was in, he might've accommodated any hard-ass cell mate who had ideas of picking a fight, and made a bad situation worse.

His one call went to Thomas Dragovich, the only lawyer he trusted enough to handle this kind of bogus charge. Dragovich didn't object to being woken up in the middle of the night; used to it after twentysome years as a criminal attorney. He listened alertly to Runyon's capsule report, asked a couple of clarifying questions, then the standard ones: Had Runyon waived his right to counsel? No, he'd refused to answer any questions without an attorney present. Had the arresting inspectors given him a bail figure? Yes, $25,000. Did they intend to contact the on-call night judge to request an increase in the amount? No, it didn't look like it. Dragovich said he'd be there as soon as he was allowed into the jail — probably not until the regular A.M. visiting hours started.

That was the way it worked out. Runyon spent four sleepless hours in the holding cell; had been pacing in tight little circles for a long time when one of the guards came and took him to an interrogation room in the main jail, where Dragovich was waiting.

The lawyer wasn't much to look at: short, slight, starting to lose his hair, his trademark gray suit, blue shirt, and loosely knotted red-striped tie looking as always as if he'd slept in them. The casual appearance was deceptive, maybe deliberately so: keep his adversaries off balance. He owned a shrewd mind and a justified reputation as one of the best trial attorneys in the city.

Dragovich had read the arrest report and the p. c. dec — the probable cause declaration — and talked to the arresting officers. "Your situation isn't as serious as it might be," he said. "The evidence they have to support the woman's claim is thin: her account of the incident, a torn dress, a statement from the security guard confirming that you were in the building, and the fingernail gouge on your neck. There's a note in the p.c. dec that she's asked for a restraining order against you, but that's standard in cases like this. The most important fact in your favor is that there are no discernible marks of violence on her person."

"Because I never touched her," Runyon said, "except to stop her from clawing my face."

"Count yourself lucky she didn't do anything to herself other than tear her clothing. Self-inflicted wounds aren't always provable as such."

"There wouldn't be a case at all if I'd thought to turn on the voice recorder when I unhooked it from her phone. Still kicking myself that I didn't."

Dragovich gestured that away.

Runyon asked, "What did the inspectors have to say?"

"Rodriguez is by-the-book, no comment, but Whitehead seems inclined to believe you after the check they ran into your background. Exemplary record as both police officer and private investigator, excellent past relationships with the SFPD and the DA's office — strong points in your favor.

They'll do everything they can to break Ms. Daniels's story. If they push her hard enough, she may decide to drop the complaint voluntarily."

"Not her. And they might have trouble breaking her. She's a compulsive liar, probably pathological — that's pretty clear now."

"And unstable, from what you told me earlier."

"Certifiable, to've come up with that extortion hoax."

"Which can work to our advantage if the case goes to trial. The more unstable an individual, the easier to discredit on the witness stand. But I'll be surprised if it goes beyond the preliminary hearing."

"And meanwhile," Runyon said bitterly, "I'm left dangling. With a suspended or revoked license, maybe."

"That's not likely to happen. In this state, only a conviction of an offense with a nexus to the professional license can be the basis for suspension or revocation by the State Board. It's possible they could get wind of the arrest and start their own investigation, but they'd have to prove misconduct according to their standards in order to take action. Most likely, in any event, they'd do nothing except wait and see if there's a conviction. Which is highly improbable in your case."

"But still possible. And the board'll get wind of the arrest, all right. Through the media, even if the cops or the DA's office don't notify them."

"Not necessarily. This isn't a high-profile matter. If there's any mention in the media at all, it won't be given much weight."

"Unless Daniels goes public, tells more lies for the attention. I wouldn't put it past her."

"Yes, that's possible," Dragovich admitted, "but we'll cross that bridge if and when we come to it."

Runyon began pacing again. "What happens now?"

"Abe Melikian has agreed to stand your bail. No collateral necessary because of your past association with him. We ought to have you out of here by mid-morning."

"I want to talk to Whitehead and Rodriguez again first. The DA's investigators, too, if you can arrange it."

"Why?"

"To make a statement, put my version of what happened last night, the whole hoax business, on the record."

Dragovich frowned. "You know you're not legally required to do that even with your attorney present. I strongly advise against volunteering information of any kind, especially in your angry frame of mind —"

"I'd just as soon do it anyway. Can you arrange it?"

". . . Yes, if you insist. And if you assure me you'll keep your emotions in check."

"Don't worry, I will."

"Very well, then." The lawyer got to his feet, stopped Runyon's pacing with a hand on his shoulder. "Two things before I go. One — I'll need as much specific information on Verity Daniels as possible, in the event of a trial. Your notes and reports on your investigation to begin with."

"I'll ask Tamara to e-mail the file to your office."

"Anything else you and Ms. Corbin can find out as well."

"You'll have it."

"Two — a caveat. I doubt you need to hear it, but I'll say it anyway. Honor the restraining order, if a judge grants it. Even if one isn't issued, you are to have nothing directly to do with Verity Daniels outside a courtroom — nothing whatsoever under any circumstances."

"Guaranteed. I wouldn't trust myself if I did."

When Dragovich was gone, Runyon prowled the room as he had the cell. Caged animal, soon to be released back into the jungle. And then what? If he lost his license, even temporarily, he'd have nothing to fill up his days, no direction, no useful purpose. For the kind of man he was, it was a hellish prospect — like being trapped in a vacuum.

It was nearly two hours before Dragovich returned with the two inspectors and an investigator from the DA's office named Sutton. None of the officers said anything, acknowledged Runyon with curt nods. Sutton, young and deceptively quiet, claimed one of four straight-backed metal chairs. Whitehead sat in a loose sprawl in another; he had a dragged-out, stale look at the tag end of his shift. Rodriguez began fiddling with the video equipment, scowling as if he were in a temper. Neither inspector could have felt half as dragged out, stale, and short-tempered as Runyon did.

The room was identical to the last one he and Dragovich had been in, when they were working to cut Bryn loose after her false confession to the murder of her son's abuser. Same metal table and chairs, same four bare walls — one of the cubicles without the two-way mirror. The only thing different from that time, and all the other times he'd been shut up inside similar inter-rogation rooms, was that now he was the one in the hot seat, with a video camera aimed at him.

For the record, Rodriguez stated the date, time, and nature of the crime, and identified Runyon, Dragovich, Sutton, Whitehead, and himself. Then they got down to it.

They let Runyon make his statement first, without interruption. He told it all in relevant detail, from his first meeting with Verity Daniels through all the steps of his manipulated investigation to the events of the night before, stressing how he received the wound on his neck.

As soon as he was finished, Sutton asked the obvious first question. "Why would a wealthy woman like Ms. Daniels concoct such a melodramatic hoax?"

"Boredom, I suppose. A way to generate some excitement in her life, get attention."

"She tell you that?"

"No. She was too furious to admit anything."

"She claims the extortion calls, all the threats are real."

"Sure she does. The rest of her story falls apart otherwise."

"You have any proof she didn't get those calls?"

"No. Not any more than she has proof that she did."

Rodriguez, leaning against the wall now with his arms folded: "Let's get back to last night. According to your story, she called and told you she'd been attacked by a masked intruder."

"That's right."

"And begged you to come to her apartment. That's the word you used, right? Begged?"

"Yes."

"Why did you go if you didn't believe her?"

"All I had at that point were suspicions," Runyon said. "It was possible she was telling the truth, and I was still working for her — I had to be sure one way or the other."

Whitehead asked, "What made you suspicious?"

"The tight security in her building, for one thing. It wasn't likely any uninvited or unannounced stranger could have gotten in. The security guard on the desk confirmed it. George something."

"Haxner. That's why you asked him all the questions about security?"

"And about Ms. Daniels's state of mind when he talked to her, yes."

Sutton: "She denies there was a man in a ski mask with a knife. Denies she called you, says it was the other way around. You called her and invited yourself over — told her you had some new information on the extortion attempt."

Runyon said carefully, "I don't lie to clients for any reason, or involve myself personally with them in any way."

"Not even good-looking women like Ms. Daniels?"

"Not anybody."

"Rich, too. Rich and attractive. Two good reasons to come on to her."

Dragovich said, "My client has already stated that he doesn't involve himself personally with his clients."

Sutton ignored him. He said to Runyon, "She says you started coming on to her from the first. More and more aggressively every time you saw or talked to her, until last night you made a direct pass. When she said no, you grabbed her and started pawing her. Told her if she didn't put out you'd walk away and let the extortionist have her."

The anger began to climb in Runyon again, bunching the muscles in his neck and across his back. "The woman is a compulsive liar —"

Dragovich gripped his arm warningly, then rose to his feet. "All right, gentlemen, we're done here. You have Mr. Runyon's statement in detail and further investigation will bear out its veracity. Unless you have a valid reason for continuing to hold him, I'll proceed with the arrangements for his bail."

Sutton shrugged and Rodriguez scowled but didn't voice an objection. Whitehead lifted himself ponderously out of his chair, stifled a yawn before he delivered the usual "keep yourself available, don't leave town" warning to Runyon. And that was the end of it for now. Runyon had been through enough interrogations to know that this one had pretty much gone in his favor, like round one of a boxing match. The inspectors and the DA's man weren't hostile, despite Sutton's prodding manner, and they'd follow up in a neutral fashion or maybe even one leaning slightly in his favor.

But that didn't make him feel any better. He had no doubt that he'd be exonerated eventually, as Dragovich had predicted, but the assault charge and arrest would still leave a smudge on his record. And there was still the looming specter of a license suspension.

An hour later he walked out of the Hall of Justice, free again but not free and clear, facing a preliminary court date in six weeks, owing Abe Melikian $2,500 for his bail and Thomas Dragovich a comparable amount in legal fees. And all because a bored,

133

conscienceless rich woman stupidly decided
to have some nasty fun at his expense.

■ ■ ■ ■

PART TWO: TAMARA

■ ■ ■ ■

10

She knew something was wrong as soon as Jake Runyon walked into her office.

Man always had the look of a business exec when he was working, neat, clean, freshly shaved. Not today. His suit and shirt were wrinkled, collar undone and tie crooked, beard stubble darkening his cheeks and chin. There was some kind of iodine-treated gash on his neck, too, angling up out of the open shirt collar. And his expression . . . grim. Real grim.

"Sorry about how I look," he said. "I spent most of the night in jail."

"Jail? Why? What happened?"

He told her. And the more she heard, the madder she got. Thoroughly pissed by the time he was through, but not at him. None of it was his fault, no matter that he tried to shoulder some of the blame. She let him know it, too. Told him he had enough to deal with without guilt-tripping himself.

"A hoax," Tamara said. "A damn stupid *game.* Where did she come up with such a wacked idea?"

"She's a TV junkie, maybe that's where."

"Well, she won't get away with it, the hoax or the phony rape charge. Case'll never get to trial. Dragovich said so, right? He's not the kind of lawyer who makes promises like that unless he's looking at a sure thing."

"It'll be on my record just the same."

"Nobody who matters will care."

"Except maybe the State Board of Licenses."

"Don't worry about that. Not likely one of their investigators will come sucking around."

"Unless Daniels goes to the media."

"Let her. It wouldn't make any difference."

"So Dragovich tells me."

"Man knows what he's talking about, right? He's got your back, so do Bill and I — all the way. You know that."

"I know it. Thanks."

"Meanwhile, business as usual."

"Sure. Business as usual."

Flat voice, flat-eyed stare — not at her, at whatever was running around inside his head. Still dumping on himself, probably. She felt sorry for him, an almost maternal kind of sympathy. Yeah, right, maternal. Earth Mother Tamara, who'd never even come close to having or wanting kids. Besides, the man was almost as old as Pop.

"Listen," she said, "why don't you take the day off, get some sleep. Come back to work tomorrow fresh —"

"Sleep and time alone aren't what I need right now. I'll stop by my apartment, shower off the jail stink and change my clothes, then get back to work."

"On what?"

"The Patterson skip-trace. I'm through with Daniels, on advice of counsel."

"Better that way. She's my meat from now on."

When Jake was gone, Tamara sat fuming for a time before she called Bill to tell him the news. She hated to bug him with a thing like this, when he had so much to deal with at home, but he'd want to know.

Pissed him off just as much as it did her. He said, "Just when you think you've come up against every kind of crazy there is. Hell of a thing. How's Jake holding up?"

"Okay, but he's blaming himself."

"Not his fault."

"I told him that. Still says he should've seen it coming."

"So should we, comes to that. But you

always give the client the benefit of the doubt when there're threats involved. I wouldn't have handled it any differently. Neither would Alex or any other investigator."

"Told him that, too."

"The rape charge won't hold up once the extortion claim is exposed for what it is."

"If it's exposed."

"It will be. Too many holes in both stories. Jake'll come out of it all right, license intact."

"He's worried the arrest'll still be on his record."

"It won't be for long. We'll help him get a judge to expunge it."

"Bitch is liable to put him through a lot more grief before anything's resolved. What the hell kind of woman is she, anyway?"

"The sick kind."

"Yeah, well, she'll be a lot sicker if I have anything to say about it. Jake's staying clear of her now, but I'm thinking maybe I ought to put Alex on her case, see if he can turn up anything that might help."

"Not a good idea," Bill said, "at least not right now. If Daniels goes any further off the rails, then yes. But right now we're better off staying clear. Let the police handle it, see what develops."

Tamara knew he was right, but the idea of doing nothing chafed at her after the conversation ended. So did the mystery of Verity Daniels's character, or lack of one. Compulsive liar, sure. Vindictive, sure. Bored rich bitch, no interests aside from the boob tube, bland personality, lousy track record with men . . . but none of that quite explained what made her tick. Or what she got out of making up all that bullshit about extortionists, knife-wielding dudes in ski masks, sexual advances and attempted rape. A few cheap TV-movie thrills, or was there more to it than that?

Tamara spent some Net time checking on compulsive/pathological liars, the distinctions between that type of individual and the true sociopath. Lot of information, but not enough to suit her. So then she called Dr. David Zinberg, her psych professor when she'd been at S.F. State. Dr. Zinberg had retired a couple of years back, and been willing once before, on a different type of case, to let her pick his brain. Luckily she caught him home and not too busy to talk. He was his usual mildly irascible self — on the phone, in person, in the classroom, always the same.

"You're not going to quote me on anything I say, are you, Ms. Corbin? Or require me to testify in court?"

Tamara smiled a little. Those were the same things he'd asked before agreeing to the previous Q&A. Cautious old guy, jealous of his time, and concerned that something might interfere with his retirement pursuit — writing "a definitive biography" of some obscure French contemporary of Freud.

"No, sir," she said. "Strictly for my own information. Trying to understand the psychological makeup of a certain type of person."

"Proceed, then."

She laid out Verity Daniels's pattern of behavior, including the extortion hoax but without going into specifics or stating gender — keeping it general, hypothetical. "What would you say is wrong with a person like that, Doctor?"

"I can't answer that question without certain knowledge of the subject's family and medical history. However, an educated guess is that the compulsion to lie and concoct elaborate fabrications is a form of the umbrella term CPI. That is, constitutional psychopathic inferiority. Generally speaking, mental illness in which an individual's lack of a moral center produces social discord."

"Born that way? Some sort of genetic quirk?"

Dr. Zinberg sighed. "Inherent in the person's basic nature, yes. And perhaps exacerbated by a difficult childhood — neglect, lack of social interaction, loneliness. A child's cry for attention perverted by circumstances as the person grows into adulthood. That is all the speculation I'm willing to indulge in, Ms. Corbin. Academic questions only, please."

"Compulsive liars tell lies regardless of the situation, right?"

"Correct. Lying, distorting the truth about both large and small issues is habitual to them, literally a way of life. They take comfort in it — it feels right to them. Whereas they find telling the truth difficult, uncomfortable."

"Sort of like an addiction."

"It *is* an addiction," Dr. Zinberg said. "In the same sense that drugs or alcohol or sexual promiscuity are an addiction to individuals seeking satisfaction on the one hand, escape from disagreeable or painful matters on the other. Lying provides a safety net, and in so doing makes the person increasingly bold and reinforces the compulsion to tell even more lies."

"Do they believe the lies they tell?"

"Oh, yes. Absolutely. Belief is part of the safety net, necessary in order to self-justify the compulsion. The larger, more complicated the fabrication, the greater the individual's need to believe in it."

"Plus it gets them more attention, feeds their egos."

"Yes."

"Sort of along the lines of Munchausen by proxy."

"No, Ms. Corbin. You mustn't confuse those who have Munchausen by proxy with the constitutional psychological inferior who compulsively lies. The illnesses have similarities but they are not the same. The compulsive liar is afflicted by narcissistic personality disorder or by borderline personality disorder."

"What's the difference between the two?"

"Both the narcissist and the borderline are individuals whose entire world revolves around their own needs and desires. Lies, deception, little or no concern for others and how their behavior affects others are symptomatic of both. The primary difference is that the narcissist is so involved with his own self-image that he buries his emotions entirely. The borderline is concerned with his immediate needs and has no control over his emotions, though he is capable of a limited amount of empathy, if and only if, it pertains to him. In the narcissist's universe, others are no more than dependent satellites. The borderline's universe is often deliberately fused with that of others, for as long a period as the individual finds it suitable or beneficial."

"So it'd be the borderline who's capable of making up intricate hoaxes for their own amusement?"

"Yes. Amusement, gratification, pleasure."

"Sexual pleasure? If it was part of the fantasy?"

"Yes."

"And after a time the fantasy becomes totally real to them? Like the other lies they tell?"

"Precisely."

"Suppose the borderline is found out, confronted? How would they react?"

"BPDs, like NPDs, are fearful of abandonment and prone to buildups of excessive rage when subjected to unusual strain," Dr. Zinberg said. "When faced with the threat of abandonment, the narcissist takes the initiative and abandons first, while the borderline clings until actually abandoned. Then typically, the individual loses control and turns on the offending party or parties, in order to maintain the perceived safety of his world."

"How can you deal with somebody like that?"

"There is no cure for the disorder, per se. However, in some cases extensive therapy from a competent analyst —"

"No, I mean how does the average person deal with it? Is there any way you can reason with a borderline, make them understand what they're doing is wrong?"

"It might be possible, temporarily, if the BPD were in a receptive mood and saw significant benefits in a given situation. In most cases, however, their needs and desires are too tightly bound for rational discourse to have a positive result. Such an attempt, in fact, would likely have an adverse effect. It would be perceived as an attack on the BPD's universe, and be met with denial and defensive outrage."

So much for that notion.

Tamara thanked Dr. Zinberg, who reminded her again before ringing off that she mustn't use his name in any professional context. Academics. The older they got, the stranger they got — at least the ones she'd had experience with. She wondered if it was because they were a little funky to begin with or if they got that way because of all the bored, blank-eyed faces staring at them over thirty, forty, fifty years of classroom teaching, the futility of having their stored-up knowledge slide dimly in one ear and out the other. Sort of like trying to educate rooms full of zombies.

What the retired prof had told her was depressing. Verity Daniels sounded like a classic borderline loony, which would make it even harder for the cops to crack her. She'd stick like glue to the phony shakedown story and the phony rape charge. Would her hunger for attention and excitement prod her into hiring some shyster to sue Jake, sue the agency? Possible. There wasn't much chance she could win that kind of lawsuit, but you never knew what might happen in a courtroom or judge's chambers. Yeah, and fighting legal battles was expensive no matter what the outcome.

All right. Tamara pulled up the Daniels file, read through Jake's reports and her own background notes, then added what she'd learned from Dr. Zinberg. A lot of information, much of which corroborated Daniels's sickness, but there had to be more. Details on her early life. Details on the breakup of her marriage, on her relationship with Jason Avery, on the probable affair with her boss at Gateway Insurance, on other past relationships with both men and women. The more they knew about her, the better armed Jake's lawyer and the police would be. Tamara set out to see what else she could find on the Net.

Daniels had been born in Visalia, raised in a single-family home by a working mother, father unknown. Only child of an only child. No living relatives except the smart lottery winner, her mother's brother, in Ohio. Mediocre student; might not have graduated high school if even back then underachieving kids weren't being handed diplomas by underachieving school systems. No trouble in school or with the law. Moved just after graduation to Martinez, where the mother, a bookkeeper, had gotten a better-paying job. Six months after the move, mother'd been killed in an alcohol-related traffic accident and Daniels was on her own. Small life insurance policy allowed her to keep on living in the same apartment. First couple of jobs menial and short-lived: clerk at Burger King, waitress at IHOP. No reasons given for termination of employment. Had just enough typing skill to sign with an office temp employment agency. Learned enough during the year she was with them to get herself hired by Gateway Insurance in a secretarial capacity.

At Gateway eight months when she met

Scott Ostrander, place and circumstances unknown. Married him three months later, moved to Orinda. Pregnant six months after that, miscarried in the first trimester. Moved back to Martinez after the divorce. Blanks where her job at Gateway was concerned, and what if anything she'd done with her life until the relationship with Jason Avery — again, no details on how or where they'd met. Everything relevant from that point until she inherited the two million was already in the file.

How about the affair with Vincent Canaday? Anything there?

She started a backgrounder on Canaday. In the middle of it the phone rang. Joe DeFalco, an old newshound bud of Bill's who worked at the *Chronicle*. What was the skinny on Jake Runyon's arrest? Skinny. Man! Tamara restrained herself, told him tersely but quietly that there wasn't a damn bit of truth in the attempted rape charge, that it was nothing but payback by a disgruntled client. DeFalco wanted details; she put him off and he went away. No way to stop him from calling Bill, which she was sure he'd do next, but it'd get him the same answers and no more. Friggin' media vultures. There'd be others sniffing around Daniels, and she'd give them an earful, all

149

right. But the story wasn't big enough or unique enough to make a media splash, not the way she was telling it.

Back to Vincent Canaday. Born Boise, Idaho, forty-two years ago. Graduated from Eastern Washington University with a business degree. Worked for Pacific Rim Insurance in Seattle for twelve years; promoted to a minor administrative position with the company in San Francisco. Left Pacific Rim six years ago to buy Gateway Insurance — not a very wise move, judging from his and Gateway's financial standing. Married to the same woman for fifteen years, one daughter, the three of them living in a mortgaged home in Lafayette. Member of the Lafayette and Martinez Chambers of Commerce, the Kiwanis Club, and the Republican Party. No criminal record, no blemishes of any kind; man had never even had a parking ticket. No known ties to Verity Daniels beyond the fact that she'd worked for him the past two years.

In short, nothing. Canaday was the kind of pillar of the community whose public image is sacred to him, and so makes damn sure any double dealings and extramarital affairs are kept under wraps.

Tamara already had what was available on Daniels's relationships with Scott Ostrander and the Avery family. None of them seemed any more willing to provide details than Vincent Canaday; Jake's interviews bore that out. Even if she'd been inclined to go against Bill's advice, and she wasn't, sending Alex out on a field investigation would probably be a waste of time.

Reluctantly, she abandoned the notion of doing any more digging. All it would buy her was more frustration. She added the information she'd learned from Dr. Zinberg to the case file, along with a few other notes and observations, and e-mailed the file to Thomas Dragovich's law office.

11

Tamara was at her desk at eight-thirty Wednesday morning. Coming in earlier and earlier, leaving later and later — putting in ten, eleven, twelve hours six days a week now. No use fooling herself that it was just because she loved the work so much. Did love it, running a detective agency was the perfect job for her (who'd've figured?), but the reason for all the overtime was that she didn't have much of a life outside the office anymore.

Sad. Wild-ass party animal had become a workaholic and reclusive couch potato. Friendships starting to slide away because she didn't have the time or the interest in partying, making the club scene. Finally grown up, responsible, mature . . . that was what Pop and sister Claudia were saying, and maybe they were right up to a point. But there was a hollowness in her, as if parts of the old Tamara had been scooped out like the seeds and pulp from a melon, and she didn't know how to fill the void.

Vonda, her best friend since high school, said what she needed was to hook up with a quality dude — somebody like Vonda's man Ben — that'd snap her out of her funk. Yeah, sure. As if quality dudes ran in packs and all you had to do was take your pick. She'd had lousy luck with men all her life anyway — the gangsta types in high school, Horace, that asshole crook Antoine Delman. Besides, getting laid didn't seem to be as important to her as it once had. Now and then she'd feel horny, but it didn't last long, wasn't as intense like back in the day when she was horny *all* the time. Mostly she didn't even think about sex. Even the batteries in old Mr. V were dead and he was gathering dust in the drawer of her bedroom nightstand.

Sometimes she wondered if the way things were now were how they'd be for the rest of her life. All work and damn little play. Mixed feelings about that. When she was home alone, listening to music, trying to unwind with two or three glasses of wine, the idea of thirty or forty years of the same routine scared the hell out of her. But when she was in the office, doing what she did best, facing new challenges, making sure everything ran smoothly, it didn't seem like

153

such a bad deal at all. Bill had grown old doing detective work . . . well, sixties old . . . and look at him. Satisfied, content with his lot. Or he had been before Kerry got caught in all that crazy shit in Green Valley.

So what was the answer? No answer, that was the answer. You couldn't predict the future, couldn't even predict tomorrow or the rest of today. Like they always said: take it one day at a time. The future'd get here fast enough that way and then you'd know what it held for you.

The coffee she'd started on the hot plate was ready. She poured herself a cup, put one of the stale doughnuts she'd brought from home on a plate, went back to her desk, and replanted her butt in the chair. First thing to do: print out reports on a couple of completed investigations and get the invoices ready to go with them.

Just finishing that up when she heard the outer door open. Prospective client, maybe. Alex and Deron Stewart weren't due to check in in person this morning. Her office door was partly open, but she couldn't see all the way into the anteroom until she got up and went over there and pushed it open all the way.

Surprise, the nasty kind. And along with it, a sharp jolt of outraged anger.

The woman standing there, dressed in a four-figure Donna Karan suit like she'd just stepped out of a *Vogue* ad, was Verity Daniels.

No mistake: Tamara's Net searches had pulled up a couple of photographs of the woman. The anger was like a thickening weight inside her as she stepped into the anteroom. Daniels stood at ease, bright red mouth not quite smiling, watching her out of eyes black-rimmed with too much mascara and Latisse-lengthened lashes. The lashes looked like a couple of spiders clinging to purple-rouged lids.

They stood there measuring each other, Tamara telling herself to stay cool, stay cool, let Daniels snap the silence and don't say anything to provoke her.

After about ten seconds: "You're Tamara Corbin?"

"That's right."

"I didn't know you were black. Or that you were so young."

Two remarks that Tamara didn't much like hearing from anybody. Coming from this nutcase, they were a plain damn insult. She said, "So what?" in a voice sharper and more combative than she'd intended.

"Nothing, I suppose. It's just that you're not what I expected."

"You're what I expected."

"Really? And what would that be?"

It was on the tip of Tamara's tongue to tell her. She managed to curb the impulse, said instead, "What do you want here, Ms. Daniels?"

"Oh, so you know who I am."

"Who you are, and what you are."

"Well, so you're going to be nasty. I was hoping we could have a reasonable discussion."

"Reasonable. After what you did to Jake Runyon?"

"I didn't do anything to him, except call the police after he tried to attack me —"

"Bullshit."

One corner of Daniels's mouth turned down. "Vulgar," she said. "Well, that's typical, isn't it."

"Of what? An uppity young black woman?"

"You said it, I didn't. I'm not a bigot."

The rage was starting to choke Tamara. She felt herself giving in to it, couldn't keep from saying, "No, just a liar, a fraud, a crazy who gets her kicks making up stories about extortionists and guys with knives and attempted rapes that never happened."

"I'm none of those things, Ms. Corbin. And I resent being told I'm crazy. I'm as sane as you are."

"Like hell. You belong in a wack shack."

Daniels drew herself up. Indignant now, or pretending to be, but still with her cool in check. Cool? Dry ice was more like it. The kind of female that eats her young. You couldn't shake her with hard truths any more than you could reason with her. The protective force field she'd built up around that private world she lived in was too thick.

"I hired your agency," she said, "because I was terrified of the person who keeps harassing me, demanding money and making terrible threats. I still am, whether you believe it or not. For your information, he called again last night."

"More bullshit. Nobody called you, not last night, not ever. Nobody's after you. H-o-a-x, hoax."

"You're just like Runyon, aren't you? Only pretending to be on my side. Neither of you really cares about helping someone in trouble, you're just out for all you can get. Sex, money, whatever. Well, you won't get away with it any more than he will."

"You threatening me now?"

"I came here thinking you might be decent enough to apologize —"

"Sure you did."

"— but you've been as crude and ugly to

157

me as he was. You don't leave me any choice, Ms. Corbin."

"Let me guess. Suing us for damages."

"Yes. You deserve it, both of you."

"That the truth or another one of your lies?"

"I have every right to protect myself legally. I've already hired an attorney."

"One of those sleazeball dudes who advertises on television, I'll bet. What's his name?"

"I don't have to tell you that now."

"How much you after? Not that you'll ever see any of it."

"Or that, either. You'll find out when the time comes."

"Yeah. And that's the real reason you're here. Tell me to my face you're suing, whether it's true or not, and watch me squirm. Only you don't get the satisfaction because I don't squirm."

"You will." Smiling now, a red gash of a smile as if her mouth was filled with blood. "Oh, you *will*."

"This how you get your jollies? Trying to ruin innocent people with all your goddamn lies? Sure it is. Better than fingering yourself under the bed covers."

That got a reaction. Daniels's smile disappeared; her eyes sparked hot under those

Latisse spiders, spots of color bloomed in her cheeks. "God, you're vulgar."

"You already said that."

"Vulgar and disgusting."

"That's me, all right." Tamara was so furious now she was shaking. "And if you don't haul that chubby ass of yours out of here in the ncxt thirty seconds, you'll find out what else I can be."

Daniels used up ten of the thirty seconds in a stone-cold glare, then turned on her spike heels and yanked open the door. Turned back again there, and showed what the thing that lived inside that closed-off universe of hers was really like, same as she had to Jake two nights ago. Said hard and fast through peeled back lips and clamped teeth, "Fucking bitch."

"Right back at you."

The door slammed on the last word, hard enough to have shattered glass.

Tamara stormed back into her office, sat down with her hands gripping her thighs. Sat like that for five minutes or so until she calmed down. Handled the woman all wrong, she thought then. Bill was always after her to keep her emotions under control, be professional no matter what the circumstances. She listened to him, she understood the need, but she couldn't seem to learn. Times like this, when she had somebody like Verity Daniels confronting her, ragging on her, the dark side of her nature took over and she just plain lost it.

Not that it made a whole lot of difference in this case. She could've been all sweetness and light, kissed Daniels's ass, and the result would've been the same. Another pack of lies . . . maybe. Some shyster lawyer already hired . . . maybe. Lawsuits in the works, the woman intending all along to play her malicious payback game to a different audience . . . maybe. How the hell could you tell ahead of time?

Well, whatever the loony was up to, she'd got a whole lot more than she bargained for walking in here today.

Now she had a pissed-off tiger by the tail.

Tamara didn't call Bill to report the confrontation with Daniels, and she didn't tell Jake about it when he checked in briefly in the late afternoon. Both of them had enough grief to deal with as it was. Why heap any more until it was necessary? There was still a chance the cops would expose Daniels for the sick liar she was, and Jake would be cleared and the whole miserable business would just fade away. If that didn't happen and Daniels went through with her lawsuit threat, there'd be time enough to plan strategy when her shyster crawled out of his hole.

Same went for hiring an attorney to represent Jake and the agency. Charles Kayabalian was one option; he and Bill were tight, had worked together on several cases. If he couldn't handle it himself, he'd recommend a legal pit bull with just as much bite. Claudia could probably recommend somebody, too, even though her specialty was corporate law, but Tamara didn't want to confide in big sister if she could help it. She'd get the usual lecture along with a list of names. Claudia was okay most of the time, but the two of them were polar opposites — Ms. Prim and Proper versus the Tiger Woman — and when it came to the old combination of Tamara and trouble, Claudia could be so tight-assed she squeaked.

Wait and see. That was the best approach right now.

Tamara stayed late again that night. What was the point of trading an empty office for an empty Potrero Hill crib? The only difference was, the flat had some food and a couple of bottles of Chardonnay chilling in the fridge. But if she got hungry or thirsty enough, she could always walk across the square to the South Park Café.

Quarter to seven when she finished the last of her work. Now she had the names of two civil rights attorneys, both of whom had won far more cases than they'd lost. Neither one came cheap, but money wasn't a consideration in something like this. You got what you paid for. And the stakes they'd be playing for here were bound to be high.

Gritty eyestrain had begun to blur her vision, as always happened when she'd spent too many hours staring at the screen on her Mac. She rubbed her eyes clear, yawned, logged off and shut down, yawned again, picked up her purse, and dragged her booty out of the chair.

And the phone screeched at her.

Now what? New or old client, she hoped. Even a wrong number or a misguided telemarketer would be okay. Just no more bad news. She'd had more than enough of that for one day.

She picked up, gave the agency's name. And a familiar voice said, "Tamara? Good, I caught you in. I thought you might be working late when I didn't get an answer at your home number."

A feeling both cold and hot flowed

through her. She didn't say anything.

"It's me, Tam," he said. "It's Horace."

12

Horace.

Out of the dead past, like a voice from the grave.

"Tam? It's been a long time —"

"Yeah."

"— and I know you're surprised to hear from me after the way things ended with us —"

"What you calling for, man?"

"I'd like to see you, talk to you."

"Talking now, aren't you?"

"No, I mean in person."

"Oh, yeah, sure. About as much chance of me coming to Philly as flying to the moon."

"Not here. Out there." Plaintive note in his voice. Working her for some damn reason? "I'll be in S.F. next week."

"No," she said. "I don't want to see you."

"Tam, listen, it's not what you think. It's not a business or pleasure trip. And I'm not looking to hit on you."

"Wouldn't do you any good if you tried."

"I'm moving back," he said.

Blink. "Moving back. Why?"

"Got nowhere else to go, now."

"Yeah? What happened to your gig with the philharmonic?"

"Lost my seat. Little over a month ago."

"Screwed it up somehow, I suppose."

"No, it wasn't my fault."

"Nothing's ever your fault, right?"

"They liked my playing, but the conductor decided to go with a more experienced cellist from New York. I tried to get on with another orchestra back here, but none of them are hiring."

Tamara was silent.

"There's a chance I can get on with the S.F. Symphony," Horace said. "If not . . . well, my other options are better out there and San Francisco's home. You know I never did like the East Coast much."

I don't know anything about you, she thought. Not when we were together, not now.

"Besides, I can crash with Charley Phillips for a while. You remember Charley?"

"Married and has a kid."

"There's a rec room in his basement he says I can use for a nominal rent."

"Ought to be real cozy for you and what's

her name, the violinist you hooked up with back there."

"Mary and I aren't together anymore."

That funny cold-and-hot feeling went through her again. "No? Last time we talked, two of you were all hot for each other and getting married."

"We did get married. It . . . just didn't work out."

The old Tamara would've been pleased. But the news just rolled off her now. "Well, you won't be alone for long," she said. "Not you. But don't get any ideas about crawling back with me. Ain't gonna happen. Dump me once, you don't get a second chance."

"I wasn't thinking that way. I know how badly I hurt you —"

"Like hell you do."

"Tam, we all make mistakes and leaving you was the biggest of my life. I know that now, and I know it's too late to do anything about it. But can't we just sit down together and talk when I get back?"

"Got nothing more to say to each other."

"I don't believe that."

"Better believe it. No more rapping now, I'm busy. Good-bye, have a nice new life."

"Wait! Don't hang up."

She waited, but she didn't take her finger off the disconnect button.

166

"I'm going to need wheels," he said. "Mary got the car we had here and I can't afford to buy even a junker out there. I hate to ask you, but . . . I'd like to have my old Toyota back."

"You bastard. So that's the real reason you called."

He said, quick, "No, no, don't misunderstand. It's just that I'm in a pretty bad financial bind. I don't want to keep my car, just use it until I find a job and can afford —"

"*Your* car? You damn well gave it to me when you took off for Philly."

". . . I thought we agreed you'd take care of it for me until I needed it again."

"That's not the way I remember it. 'Keep the car, Tamara, I won't need it anymore.' "

"When did I say that?"

"Last time we talked, when you told me about falling in love with Mary from Rochester. Three years and not a word since, and now you need the frigging car again and I'm supposed to just hand over the keys when you show up."

Wheedling note in his voice now. "You've got a good job, you're a full partner in that agency —"

"How'd you know that?"

"I've kept track of you, I never stopped

caring, whether you believe it or not." Pause. "You can afford to buy another car, can't you?"

"I already did, six months ago," she lied.

"Good, good. Then you won't mind letting me have the Toyota."

"Not if I still had it."

"What? But you couldn't have sold it, it's registered in my name."

"Was. You're forgetting something, man."

"Forgetting what?"

"You signed the pink slip over to me."

And she jabbed the disconnect button before he could say anything more.

It was nearly eight o'clock when she keyed open the front door to her flat and dragged her tired ass up the stairs. The flat took up the entire second floor of a refurbished Stick Victorian on Connecticut Street, six rooms plus bath and attic — too big for one person, really. Scooted around from room to room like a mouse in a maze. She'd loved it at first, considered herself lucky to snag digs like this for what, by city standards, was a reasonable rent. But it hadn't been the same since Antoine Delman busted in and tried to kill her. She'd *really* been lucky that night — lucky to be still alive.

All the damage had long since been repaired, but Tamara couldn't go into the dining room without feeling a chill, and she stayed out of the attic entirely. Delman hadn't died here, but it was as if his ghost haunted the place just the same. She'd have moved by now, except that it would've meant breaking the lease. Landlord was still pissed at having to replace the insulation and the dining room ceiling and wouldn't cut her any slack, so she was stuck here until the lease was up.

For a while after the Delman nightmare, being alone here at night gave her the willies. Not so much anymore. Most of the time now the ghost didn't walk and the place was almost as comfortable as it'd been in the beginning; she could relax and sleep without waking up and listening for imaginary bumps in the night. The flat was the nicest place she'd ever lived outside of the folks' home in Redwood City. A whole lot nicer than the apartment on 27th Avenue she'd shared with Horace, then occupied by herself when he split for Philadelphia.

Horace.

Another damn ghost come back to haunt her.

Cold in the flat tonight, even though she'd left the furnace on at sixty-five. She turned the thermostat up to seventy, tossed her coat on the couch, and went into the kitchen. She'd been hungry before Horace's call; wasn't hungry anymore. Poured herself a big glass of wine, all she wanted now. Took it into the bedroom, then into the bathroom after she undressed.

She felt better after a long, hot shower had loosened some of the kinks in her neck and shoulders. While she was toweling dry, she caught a glimpse of herself in the steamy full-length mirror. Rubbed the glass clear for a better look. Not bad. Kept the promise to herself not to put back any of the weight she'd lost; food just didn't interest her much anymore. Not exactly a hard body now, but as slim and trim as she'd ever been in her life. Thirty pounds less than she'd weighed when she'd been with Horace —

Horace again.

He'd love the way she looked now. Wouldn't be able to keep his big hands off her boobs and the rest of her.

"No way, baby," she said aloud. "Never gonna see or touch *this* naked body again."

She put on her robe, finished her wine, went to the kitchen to pour another glass. Too quiet in there; she put on a CD without paying any attention to what it was. Sat on the couch with the music swirling around her and the wine warm in her throat and belly.

Damn Horace. Why'd he have to lose his seat on the Philadelphia Philharmonic, have his marriage to Mary from Rochester bust up? Why couldn't he just stay away from San Francisco?

He wouldn't leave her alone; foregone conclusion she'd hear from him again. Bug her about getting together. Bug her about the Toyota when he found out she'd lied to him about selling it. And he would find out, somehow, some way. Another foregone conclusion.

God, she hated that car. Thirteen years old now, red paint job starting to fade and crack, engine needing work more and more often, brakes wearing out, tires out of alignment again. A frigging hand-me-down with that stupid MR CELLO license plate. She'd been promising herself for a long time now to trade it in on a new ride. Why hadn't she done it? Could have real easy; he *had* signed the pink slip over to her, no lie there. Well, it wasn't for any sentimental reason that she hadn't sold it. Too busy, too lazy. And now it was too late.

No, it wasn't. Go right out tomorrow and trade the Toyota in on something new or at least newer. He couldn't stop her. Serve him right, for what he'd done to her, all the crap he'd laid on her long-distance two years ago. She still remembered every word of that conversation, also delivered to her while she was at work.

Hardest thing I've ever had to do is make this call . . . hate to have to hurt you, I'm so sorry . . . didn't want it to happen, neither Mary nor I did . . . wish to God it could have turned out differently for you and me . . . never stop loving you, Tamara, want only the best for you . . .

And tonight, more of the same.

Maybe she ought to just let him have the Toyota. It was *his* piece of crap, after all — he deserved to be stuck with it. She could afford to buy a car of her own. Give him what he wanted and then he'd go away and leave her in peace, wouldn't he?

Not necessarily. Not old horny Horace, on the prowl now that he was divorced or getting divorced. One thing they'd always had together was good sex. Oh Lord yes, great sex — best she'd ever had, no use denying that. There were times when she —

Knock it off, girl. None of that kind of thinking.

You don't want him back, not for any reason. You wouldn't take him back if he crawled all the way down Market to the

172

Ferry Building to beg you.

Dead, you and Horace. As dead as you and Antoine Delman.

More important things in your life now. Much more important. The agency and how you've made it grow and prosper. Crazy clients and potential lawsuits. You don't need a love life right now — it's the last thing you need. Too many complications. Wouldn't even want a relationship with a quality dude like Vonda's Ben. And Horace sure as hell isn't a quality dude by any stretch. Was once, maybe, but not anymore. Not anymore.

Quit thinking about him!

13

The next two workdays were quiet. Verity Daniels didn't show up at the agency or call on the phone or bug Jake anymore. Horace didn't call again. Things ran smoothly, in a normal routine. Nothing happened on the weekend, either. Tamara spent part of Saturday in the office, left earlier than usual because Vonda and Ben had invited her to a party and she figured she might as well go. Too much time alone just wasn't good for her mental health, especially now with the personal and professional hassles still unresolved.

The party was okay. Mixed group, black like Vonda, white and Jewish like Ben. Couple of unattached guys looking for dates, one of each color, the black dude paying more attention to Tamara than any of the other singles. He wasn't bad looking, seemed nice enough, but he talked too much about himself and his job, something to do with industrial chemistry that he thought was fascinating and she didn't. Sure no chemistry between them, and that was just as well. She just didn't need another potential complication in her life right now.

Sunday she drove over to Golden Gate Park, spent the morning wandering around Stow Lake and then the Academy of Sciences, and that would've been okay, too, except that while she was eating lunch in a restaurant on Irving, a brother dressed like a pimp kept trying to hit on her. Men. All the same when they spotted a woman alone and got a whiff; you could almost see this dude's nostrils twitch. He even followed her out and tried out his sorry-ass line again on the sidewalk. A real jerk. So then she went home and used up the rest of the day and evening reading and napping in bed, glad to be alone again.

Back in the office bright and early Monday morning, looking forward to another quiet, routine day. And that was just what it was, until eleven-thirty. Then it all went to hell.

The guy who walked in was in his twenties, a smiley-face in a suit and tie and carrying a briefcase and a manila envelope. Didn't look like a potential client, and wasn't. He said, "Ms. Corbin? Tamara Corbin?" and when she admitted it, he handed

175

her the papers, said, "You have a nice day now," and left her standing there with her mouth open.

Process server.

Daniels's lawsuit threat was genuine.

Tamara sat down in her office and waded through the papers. The lawyer's name was Hansen, Philip Hansen, nobody she'd ever heard of; his address — Green Street, low number, which put it near the Embarcadero — didn't tell her anything, either. She skipped most of the legalese, looking for the gist of the complaint. There: plaintiff seeking damages for grievous personal distress owing to negligence, incompetence, and slander in the sum of . . . holy Jesus! . . . $250,000.

Big money the bitch didn't need, probably didn't even want. She wasn't playing this liar's game for fun, but out of pure malice.

For three or four minutes Tamara stalked the office until her fury cooled and she could think clearly again. Then she took half a dozen deep breaths, picked up the phone, and called Bill.

Charles Kayabalian's large private office in Embarcadero Center was decorated with Persian rugs, one big red-and-black one on the floor, a couple of small ones hanging on the walls. He collected Orientals, Bill had told her, and was an expert on antique Kashan and Sarouk carpets. All that meant to Tamara was that he had plenty of money, which made him a top-line attorney, which meant they were in good legal hands.

Man looked and acted successful, too. Kind of person who inspired confidence. Strong face, strong voice, smooth manner, dapper in an expensive three-piece blue suit. And calm, a lot calmer than Tamara felt. Bill was there, too, of course. And Jake. The smiley-face process server had caught him Monday evening, yesterday, at his apartment. Daniels was looking to nail him for only $100,000 in damages. *Only.*

Kayabalian had agreed to represent them as soon as Bill got in touch with him. Favor for past favors, but also because he didn't like frivolous lawsuits and enjoyed facing off against attorneys who indulged in them. He knew Philip Hansen, not personally but by reputation. Wouldn't say much against the man — professional ethics — but what he did say implied that Hansen was just what Tamara figured he was, a shyster who'd take on any kind of case on a contingency basis if the potential payoff was large enough.

"The reason for this conference," Kayabalian said when they were all seated, him behind a big mahogany desk with his hands steepled under his chin, the rest of them in facing chairs, "is to keep you informed now that I've had the chance to review both suits and the case file Ms. Corbin provided, and spoken at length with Thomas Dragovich and Ms. Daniels's attorney."

"How does our position look?" Bill asked.

"I don't have to tell you that the outcome of any civil lawsuit is difficult to predict, the more so when a jury is involved. And Hansen indicated to me that he and his client intend to request a jury trial. Nevertheless, as you indicated when we spoke on the phone, the suit against your detective agency is shaky. It would be extremely difficult for the plaintiff to prove incompetence and negligence, given your long-standing record to the contrary. We can and will call any number of witnesses to support your professional integrity."

Bill nodded and smeared a hand over his face. It had been awhile since Tamara had seen him and the way he looked worried her. Older, kind of shrunk-hunched, as if he'd aged five years in the past few months. The lines around his eyes and mouth made longer, deeper by stress. He'd lost weight, too. As thin now as he'd been since she'd known him.

"And the suit against Jake?" he asked.

"Somewhat stronger," Kayabalian said, "if the assault charge stands up. If it collapses under police investigation, or if we can prove Ms. Daniels sought your services under false pretenses, the foundations for both suits also collapse and any competent judge will toss them. In which event we can demand recompense for harassment."

"No countersuit. All we want is to get out from under."

Tamara wasn't sure she agreed with that. Why not sue the ass off Daniels for all the trouble she'd caused? But she didn't say anything. Bill was probably right; he usually was.

Kayabalian said, "If the police fail to disprove the assault charge, we'll have to hope Dragovich is able to get it dismissed at the preliminary hearing. Failing that, rely on him for an acquittal when the case comes to trial. A dismissal would certainly work in our favor; it might even convince Ms. Daniels to drop the suits. An acquittal is to our advantage only if a criminal trial were to preceed the civil."

No way she drops the suits, Tamara thought, no matter what happens with the phony rape. If she can't get Jake one way, it'll make her even more determined to do it the other.

"What are the chances of dismissal?" Bill asked.

"Dragovich is a fine criminal attorney, but . . . fairly slim, I'm afraid, despite Mr. Runyon's impeccable record for honesty. It's Ms. Daniels's word against Mr. Runyon's, and what little evidence there is supports her account of what happened that evening."

Tamara leaned forward in her chair. "What about all the evidence we've got that says she's a compulsive liar, that the extortion business was made up?"

"It's not conclusive and might be ruled inadmissible, depending on the judge. And proving the hoax won't be easy without some sort of corroborating evidence. Particularly in view of the fact that she now has alleged proof that an extortion attempt has been and is still being made."

"What proof?"

"A tape recording of the extortionist's most recent telephone call. Her attorney played it for me. Two minutes of a male voice demanding twenty thousand dollars and obscenely threatening her life if she doesn't comply, and her frightened replies."

"It's a fake. A damn fake."

"Got the idea from the recordings I tried to set up," Jake said grimly. "Bought herself a recorder and a telephone interface and paid somebody to make the call."

"I don't doubt it," Kayabalian said. "But the recording exists nonetheless, and her explanation as to why neither of the two previous calls were recorded is plausible enough. A judge may or may not rule her recording admissible — I'll certainly make every attempt to see that it doesn't happen — but you can be certain her attorney will find a way to mention its existence."

Bill said, "How much time are we looking at here before court dates are set?"

"If the assault charge stands through the preliminary hearing, a minimum of six weeks for the trial and likely much longer, given the backlog of cases on the court docket. The same applies to the civil suits."

"So we could be looking at, what, three to six months before any of this is resolved?"

"It could be that long, yes."

"And there's nothing we can do in the meantime? I mean Tamara, Jake, and me."

"No. I strongly advise all of you to have nothing whatsoever to do with Ms. Daniels or her attorney, or to conduct any sort of sub rosa investigation."

"Take the moral high road, in other words."

"Yes. Moral and legal both."

So it was back to business as usual, Tamara and Jake dealing with their shares of the agency's caseload, Bill back home to be with Kerry. But it wasn't the same business as usual for her — it was like living and working in a kind of limbo. Jake must have felt the same, but he didn't say anything about it and neither did she. You couldn't tell how he was feeling; he had that stoic way about him, like he was living behind a private wall. He seemed okay, though. Whatever was going on inside his head, it didn't affect his work; he was as efficient as always, in the office and out in the field.

Bill didn't want to talk about Daniels or the lawsuits, either. She told Alex what the situation was; as a full-time operative now, he had a right to know. But that was the only time either of them mentioned it.

The rest of the week passed with no word from the cops or anybody else involved. No news meant bad on the one hand, good on the other. And that was probably how it would play out for the duration, however many weeks or months that'd be.

Hard enough to deal with now, and it

wouldn't get any easier. The camaraderie, the usual ease in the agency routine were already missing. She was tense during the workdays, and now and then some little thing would trigger her tamped-down anger and she'd growl at a client or contact, throw or beat on something in what Claudia would've called a hissy fit. The nights weren't a whole lot better. She didn't sleep well, and once she dreamed that she came home and Horace was sitting on the couch with his arm around Verity Daniels, both of them grinning at her like a couple of Cheshire cats — an ugly dream that woke her up in a sweat. It was as if a cloud of gloom hung over her like invisible smoke.

She kept telling herself that it would all work out okay. Charles Kayabalian was a good lawyer, one of the best; they couldn't be in better legal hands. And there wasn't anything more that could go wrong between now and the court dates. The worst had already happened.

Well, hadn't it?

14

Like hell it had.

The worst happened sometime Saturday night and then on Sunday afternoon.

Tamara was lounging in bed, watching a crappy movie on TV because she had nothing better to do, when the call came in. She glowered at the phone, then at the bedside clock. Not quite two-fifteen. Better not be Horace, she thought. I'll tear him a new one if it is.

It wasn't. It was Thomas Dragovich, calling from the Hall of Justice.

He told her that in grave tones, and then he said, "I'm afraid I'm the bearer of bad news, Ms. Corbin. Jake Runyon was arrested again early this morning at his apartment."

"What! Don't tell me that Daniels woman trumped up some other charge against him —"

"Not this time. The charge is first-degree murder."

"*Murder?* Of who?"

"Verity Daniels."

". . . My God, she's dead? When, how?"

"Sometime last night," Dragovich said. "Beaten with a blunt instrument and strangled, her body dumped in Lake Merced. A jogger found it just past dawn."

The news was like being smacked with something that made you woozy, muddied your thinking. It was a few seconds before Tamara was able to wrap her mind around it. "And the cops think Jake killed her? Why, because of that phony attempted rape charge?"

"That and the lawsuits, yes."

"But that's just wacked. He wouldn't do a thing like that, not to her, not to anybody."

"Of course he wouldn't. He maintains he's had nothing to do with the woman since the confrontation in her studio, and I believe him. But he can't account for his time over the past thirty-six hours — home alone after a Saturday road trip alone."

"That's not enough to arrest him for murder!"

"No, it isn't. Not by itself. Unfortunately the police have a piece of physical evidence that directly links him to the crime, and that he can't explain to their satisfaction."

"What piece of evidence?"

"A button," Dragovich said, "clenched in the dead woman's hand. A button torn off the sleeve of a suit coat in his closet."

■ ■ ■ ■

PART THREE:
BILL

■ ■ ■ ■

15

Kerry was still holed up in her office, where she'd been ever since breakfast. I knocked on the door, then put my head inside. She was at her computer, so intent on what she was doing that she didn't seem to know I was there. The room was as gloomy as a cave with the drapes drawn and the only light coming from the monitor screen and desk lamp. Her retreat, she called it. Seven-day retreat since coming home from the hospital, for hours on end — the only place where she seemed to feel completely safe when she was alone in the condo.

I watched her for a few seconds. Outwardly she did not appear to have changed much, except that she was too thin; her color was good and her auburn hair had the same bright luster as always in the spill of light from the lamp. But up close you could see what was missing — the animation, the zest for living that had been such a vital part of her personality. Signs of returning spirit were what I kept watching for, hoping for, because it was the only way I'd know for sure that the internal wounds she'd suffered were finally healing.

Just the opposite with me. Inside I was all right, coping, but the face I saw staring back at me from the bathroom mirror every morning resembled that of an old man who'd been on a protracted bender. Maybe not quite that bad, but bad enough to make me cringe, and to put sadness and sympathy in Emily's eyes. Crises and their aftermaths have different effects on different people, the victims and those close to them both.

I went in and shut the door behind me. The click of the latch got through Kerry's concentration, led her to lift and turn her head. I said, "I need to talk to you, babe."

"I'm almost done here. Another few minutes."

That could mean ten or fifteen, or it could mean an hour or more. She seemed to have little awareness of the passage of time since July.

"It's important," I said.

"So is what I'm doing."

"It's about Jake Runyon."

"Well, what about him?"

"Bad news. Very bad. He's been arrested

again. First-degree homicide charge, this time."

She sat without moving for several seconds, her hands poised above the computer keyboard, as if she'd been flash-frozen in that position. Then she swiveled her chair so she was looking at me directly. "That's ridiculous," she said. "Jake wouldn't kill anyone in cold blood."

"I know it."

"Who? Who is he supposed to have murdered?"

"The woman who brought the bogus assault charge against him. Verity Daniels."

"My God. What happened?"

"I don't know all the details yet." I told her what I did know, from Thomas Dragovich by way of Tamara. "It's a frame job, that much is clear. The button from Jake's coat was deliberately put in Daniels's hand to implicate him."

"Who would want to do a thing like that?"

"No idea yet. Someone who hated Daniels enough to want her dead, who knew about the assault charge and figured Jake for a perfect fall guy."

"But the button. How . . . ?"

"Not stolen from his apartment — he told Dragovich he was certain there hadn't been a break-in. The only thing he can figure is that the button was torn off in his struggle with Daniels at her condo last week, that she found it or whoever killed her did."

Kerry shook her head. A shiver created a discernible ripple effect across her shoulders. "I hate this kind of thing," she said in a low voice.

"So do I."

"It makes me . . ." She let the rest of it dribble off, but I sensed what the unspoken words were; they resonated like a silent echo inside my head: ". . . even more afraid."

I let a few seconds pass before I said carefully, "Jake was there for us in Green Valley. And he was there for me a couple of times before that. I have to do the same for him now."

"Yes. Of course you do."

"It means going back to work for a while. More or less full-time until this is cleared up."

"All right."

"Tamara and I discussed it. Alex Chavez has a heavy caseload and a court appearance coming up. The only other thing we could do is hire out an investigation, but another agency wouldn't have the personal stake in it that we do."

"I said all right."

"I hate to have to leave you alone, but I

just don't see any other way. We could get someone to come in during the day —"

Wrong thing to say. Kerry slapped the desk with the flat of her hand. "For God's sake, I'm not an invalid and I'm not afraid to be alone. I don't need a nursemaid."

"I didn't mean —"

"And don't you dare let Cybil come over here. Don't even tell her you're going back to work."

We'd been over all that before. Her mother had offered several times to move in temporarily, to help with Kerry's recuperation, but it wouldn't have been a good idea even if Cybil's health had permitted it. Or possible, for that matter, because we didn't have room to put her up. In her frail condition and showing signs of age-related dementia, it was Kerry who'd have had to care for her instead of the other way around.

"Don't worry," I said, "I won't do anything you don't want me to."

The little fit of anger died as suddenly as it had flared up. Her expression altered to one of contrition; she stood up, came around the desk to stand in front of me. Not touching, which meant she didn't want to be held, but close enough so that I could smell the sweetness of her breath.

"I'm sorry," she said. "I know it's hard for

you, too. Worse now with Jake in trouble. But you do what you have to do for him and let me do what I have to do for me. Okay?"

"Okay."

Brief wan smile, brief touch on my arm. "I feel so sorry for Jake," she said. "Help him. Any way you can."

I nodded.

You, too, *mia amore,* I thought. Any way I can.

Emily came home at six, after a day out with a friend at some sort of pop concert. Kerry was still in her office, which gave me a chance to talk privately to the kid while the two of us fixed dinner.

Kid? No, that was no longer accurate. Just fourteen, sure, but a lot of pain and adversity had been crammed into those fourteen years — the painful loss of both of her parents, her mother a victim of sudden violence, and all the crap Kerry and I had been through separately and together since we'd adopted her. Less bright, less adaptable girls her age might have suffered irreparable psychological damage. Not Emily. Each incident had made her stronger, hastened her maturity until now she seemed to me more grown up than women two and three times her age.

Beautiful girl, too, already filling out into womanhood; by the time she was twenty-one she'd be stunning. But her beauty wasn't now nor would it ever be the brittle, egocentric kind you saw so much of these days. She'd turn heads, but she'd never allow hers to be turned: I had no doubt she'd make the right choices when it came to education, love, career. If there was any justice in this world, she'd be the singer she dreamed of being, have all the other good things she wanted out of life. No one deserved it more.

I'd never treated or talked to her as a child, and I didn't now. I explained the situation with Jake Runyon in detail, including the conversation I'd had with Kerry earlier, and when I was finished she paused to consider before she said, "I think Mom will be okay here alone most of the day."

"Well, she seems to think she will."

"It might even be a good thing. For her, I mean."

"Why do you say that?"

"She has to learn not to be afraid anymore. It's the only way she's going to get back to her old self."

"That's right, it is. And she is learning, slowly."

"Maybe it wouldn't be so slow," Emily said, "if we weren't making her dependent on us."

That surprised me a little. "You think we're making her dependent?"

"I don't know. Maybe. We're always kind of walking on eggshells around her — doing things for her, trying to get her to do things for herself. That could be why she spends so much time in her office."

"Then why hasn't she said anything?"

"Because it's easier not to. And because she wasn't ready to."

"But now you think she might be?"

"Don't you, Dad? After what she said when you told her you were going back to work?"

Smart girl, Emily. Twice as smart as I'll ever be.

I could only hope she was right this time.

Kerry had little to say at dinner, but at least she didn't retreat into her office afterward. The three of us watched a movie, again mostly in silence, but that was all right because the two hours sitting together in semidarkness had some of the old sense of family closeness we'd shared previously. Maybe it was wishful thinking, but the strain and tension that I'd felt on so many

196

recent evenings like this seemed mostly absent.

Same in our bedroom later. More silence from Kerry, but not the uncomfortable kind. And just as I was starting to doze, I heard and felt her rustling around on her side of the bed, then she was there beside me, her arms sliding around my body and turning it so that it fitted tightly against hers. But it wasn't like the other nights when I'd awakened to find her clinging desperately to me in the darkness. Those nights she'd wanted only to be held. Those nights she'd been wearing her nightgown and tonight, now, she wore nothing.

"Make love to me," she said against my chest.

I was wide awake by then. But hesitant, uncertain. "Are you sure?"

"Yes. Please."

So warm in my arms, but still I held her gingerly, my hands unmoving on her bare flesh. "If you'd rather we can just hold each other —"

"Hush." Her hands were the ones that moved, urgently — caressing, seeking. "There, that's it. Yes, good. No more talking now. Just make love to me."

It started slow, like always with us, but it was too slow for Kerry. Too gentle, too tender. What she wanted, demanded, was like a collision. Over too quickly for me, and so intense for her at the end that she made a sound almost like a muffled shriek of pain.

Afterward, almost immediately, she edged away to her side of the bed and turned on her side, facing away from me. And huddled there, she began to cry. Silent weeping, the most heartbreaking a man can endure from the woman he loves.

16

They wouldn't let me see Runyon. No visitors allowed, I was told at the main jail, except for the prisoner's attorney. Lockdown, because of his law enforcement ties? Either that, or Administrative Segregation dictated by the nature of the crime.

I called Thomas Dragovich's office on my cell, but he wasn't in; his secretary said he had a court date this morning. So then I went down to the Homicide Division to see if I could get an audience with the investigating officers. Nothing doing there, either. They were out in the field and none of the other inspectors would discuss the case with me.

Not like the old days, when I knew several ranking cops from my own time on the force and could have called in a favor. Eberhardt, once a lieutenant in General Works, who'd been a close friend and later my partner before he screwed up his life — and mine for a while — with bad decisions. Jack Logan, the last of the old guard, who'd risen to assistant chief before yet another departmental shake-up not long ago had forced him to retire. Casual and nodding acquaintances with a handful of others over the years who might have been able to pull a string for me, now also gone. Victims of time and change, like me, like all of us.

From the Hall of Justice I drove to South Park. Tamara was in her office, and when I went in there she said, "You talk to Jake?"

"No. No visitors yet except his attorney. And Dragovich is in court today. I'll just have to wait . . . unless Kayabalian knows somebody at the Hall who can get me a few minutes with Jake."

"I just got off the phone with him — Kayabalian. Thought he should know the score right away."

"What did he say?"

"Well, the good news is that we're off the hook on the civil suits. Daniels had no heirs to carry them on, and there's no case without her anyway. If we can get Jake off the hook, too, then we'll come out of this mess pretty clean. Woman did us a favor getting herself knocked off."

"You call being beaten and strangled a favor?"

"She deserved what she got."

"Come on, Tamara, show a little compassion. Nobody deserves to die by violence. Nobody."

"Okay. But how much compassion did she show Jake? And you and me and most of the other folks in her miserable life?"

Too young to be so cold, callous, bitter, even if there was a certain amount of justification here. But it was not the time or place to deliver a lecture on humanity. I said, "How long ago did you talk to Kayabalian?"

"Few minutes."

"So he should still be in his office."

He was. "As Runyon's attorney in the civil matter," he said when I got through to him, "I may be able to get you an audience with him. I'll see what I can do and get back to you."

"Thanks, Charles."

"Don't thank me yet." Pause. Then, with mild censure in his voice, "Are you as happy as your partner that my legal services will no longer be required?"

"No. Not at the expense of a woman's life." I was in my office with the connecting door to Tamara's office closed, so she couldn't hear what I said next. "Tamara's young and still learning. Everything including justice is black and white to her — and that's not a pun."

"Mm. I remember what it was like to be young," he said wryly. "And most of the time, professionally speaking, I'm glad I'm not anymore."

"Me, too," I agreed. "Most of the time."

Not long after we rang off, while I sat poring through a printout of the Daniels casefile, Runyon's lady friend, Bryn Darby, called. She'd just heard the news about Jake's arrest and couldn't believe there was any truth in it; I assured her there wasn't. Was there anything she could do? Nothing except to lend him moral support.

"Will they let me see him, do you think?"

"Depends. Maybe not right away. You'll have to check with the main jail at the Hall of Justice."

"God, that place. After what happened a few months ago . . . it gives me chills just thinking about going back there."

"I know how you feel, but it's worse for Jake now."

"Yes. You'll do everything you can for him? To get him out of there?"

"Try not to worry too much, Mrs. Darby. We're already on it."

After the call ended, I thought that Bryn Darby had sounded worried, all right, but not quite as upset as Jake had been about her when their situations were reversed. Hard to tell about something like that over the phone, but I had the feeling just the same. Things cooling down between Bryn and Jake? Not that he ever talked much about his private life, but from the way he'd gone to bat for her when she'd falsely confessed to the murder of her son's abuser, I'd assumed that they were pretty close. . . .

Back to the file. I'd looked at it before the conference in Kayabalian's office last week, but this time I paid closer attention to Runyon's reports and Tamara's search notes. None of it told me much in the way of specifics. Each of the three men in Verity Daniels's past that Jake had interviewed had cause to hate her, and it was possible his visit to one of them had stirred up old antagonisms to the point of violence. The ex-husband, Scott Ostrander? Six years was a long time to hold a killing grudge. The insurance agency owner, Vincent Canaday? Even if he had had a fling with Daniels, she didn't seem to have posed any threat to him after the inheritance move to San Francisco. The brother of her drowned fiancé looked like the best bet. But as much as Hank Avery considered her responsible for his brother's death, he hadn't made a move against her in three years. Why would he all of a sudden take his revenge now?

And the biggest question: Why frame Runyon for the murder? A revenge killing, if that was the motive, is a crime of passion; premeditation, the kind that includes diverting suspicion to someone else, doesn't usually enter into it. Any of the three could have found out about Jake's arrest on the assault charge, from Verity Daniels or in some other way, but how would any of them have gotten hold of the cuff button? Assuming Daniels had found it in her condo after the struggle, she had no reason to show it to a man she hadn't seen in months or years.

Unless she wasn't as estranged from one of the trio as she'd let on. Been seeing Canaday again, for instance. Or even her ex-husband on the sly, maybe taunting him with the promise of money from her inheritance; Ostrander's surprised emotional outburst at the nursery could've been faked for the benefit of his current wife. Daniels had been capable of just about anything; we had plenty of evidence of that.

Somebody she knew, in any case. She'd been killed somewhere other than her condo; security in that building was too tight for a violent confrontation to go unheard and uninvestigated, a dead body to be removed day or night. Lured out, then, for the purpose of killing her or for some other reason. Or she'd made the date herself and the meeting had erupted into violence.

There was another possibility, too, that I didn't want to pursue at the moment. I'd advised Tamara a few dozen times not to indulge in idle speculation, and here I was doing just that and giving myself a headache in the process. Save it until I was able to talk to Jake. Whenever that would be.

Pretty soon, as it turned out. Kayabalian called back a few minutes later to say that he'd arranged a 1:00 P.M. visit for me. "Ten minutes, that's all I could get you," he said, and I said, "That's ten minutes more than they'd give me this morning." I didn't ask him how he'd managed it; he wouldn't have told me if I had. Lawyers have their ways and means, and like the rest of us involved in one way or another with the law, they don't much like sharing them.

Runyon had already been brought into the main jail visitors' room when one of the guards escorted me in. Even through the thick Plexiglas wall that bisected the room, I could see how heavily this second unjust arrest and incarceration had worn on him. Beard stubble bristled on his cheeks and chin; his face was set in such tight, stony lines that knots and ridges of muscles were visible all along the jaw lines.

I sat down and picked up the communicating phone, watched him do the same on his side. "I tried to get in to see you this morning," I said, "but they wouldn't allow it."

"AdSeg'd me." His mouth sketched a grim smile. "Funny, isn't it. Wasn't long ago that Bryn was in here, AdSeg'd for a crime she didn't commit, and I was on the other side of the glass."

I didn't say anything. He didn't expect an answer.

"How'd you manage the visit?" he asked. "Dragovich?"

"No, he's in court today. Kayabalian. All we've got is ten minutes."

"Yeah, they told me."

"Wanted you to know that I'm on it, Jake. Tamara, too. With or without police cooperation, for as long as it takes."

"Kerry . . . ?"

"Not a problem. She's okay with it."

He nodded.

"Daniels," I said. "Any idea who killed her, and why?"

"Somebody from her past, that's all I can figure. She didn't seem to have much of a present."

"Pretty secretive, though, wasn't she? And an adept liar. She could've been involved with somebody — a married man, say — and kept it on the QT."

"Yeah, possible."

"She drop any names to you besides the ones in your report? Even just a first name?"

"Not that I remember. No."

"Have to ask you this, Jake: Any chance she was telling the truth about the extortion attempt? That she really was being pressured by an anonymous caller?"

"I thought of that, too. No. It was a hoax, all right." One corner of his mouth bent upward, not so much a humorless smile this time as half a rictus. "That's about the only thing I'm sure of right now."

"So it's odds against her murder being connected to the hoax, or the phony assault charge and the lawsuits."

"Except in the minds of the cops."

"Which leaves fear, revenge, greed."

"Fear or revenge, if it's somebody from her past. Lot of people had cause to hate her."

"But why now? Something had to trigger it."

"Could be me showing up, asking questions, delivering information," Runyon said. "Her ex-husband didn't know about her inheritance. Neither did Hank Avery."

"Either of them give you a hard time?"

"No."

"The insurance man, Canaday?"

"No."

"What I can't figure is the frame," I said. "Why would anybody from Daniels's past or present want to implicate you? Can't see it as a grudge. Just a convenient fall guy?"

"Has to be. That damn button . . . Daniels must've ripped it off my coat in that little skirmish we had."

"You didn't notice it was missing?"

"No. Old suit I don't wear much, blood on the collar where she scratched me — I noticed that — so I just dropped it on the pile for the cleaners and forgot about it."

"Daniels must have found the button," I said, "but not until after she'd made the phony assault charge. Otherwise she'd have turned it over. Question is, why did she keep it? Souvenir?"

"More likely to give it to her lawyer, have him use it against me in the court cases."

"Another question: how did the killer get hold of it? Any reason you can think of why she'd give it to anybody? Or even tell anybody she had it?"

"No."

I glanced at my watch; not much time left.

208

"The police give you any idea when she was last seen?"

"One of the security men saw her leave the Bayfront Towers garage at four-thirty Saturday afternoon. He was the last so far."

"What about her car? You know if it's been found?"

"No. They wouldn't tell me."

"When you were out driving on Saturday, where'd you go?"

"North. Napa County, Lake Berryessa. Nothing else to do, I take long drives."

"Stop anywhere? Talk to anyone?"

"For gas in Napa. And when I got back to the city, a Chinese restaurant on Clement for takeout."

"What time was that?"

"Six-thirty, seven. No help there. She wasn't killed until around ten — one of the homicide inspectors told me that. I was home by then, no visitors, no calls. And I didn't go out again."

"Nothing incriminating in your car and your apartment, they know that by now. The only real evidence against you is that button."

"Found clenched in her dead hand. Enough to keep me locked up and enough for a conviction, we both know that."

The guard on Runyon's side of the Plexiglas came walking over to call time. Fast ten minutes. I said, "I'll be in touch, Jake, in person or through Dragovich." I wanted to say more, something reassuring, but he'd already put the phone down. Just as well, I thought as the guard led him away. Anything I might have said would've sounded just like what it was: cold comfort.

17

The rest of Monday was a scramble. From the Hall of Justice I drove to Bayfront Towers to see if I could find out anything from the day-shift security staff about Daniels's movements and recent visitors. Then I went to the agency to confer with Tamara and look over the additional information she'd dug up on Scott Ostrander, Vincent Canaday, and the Averys. Then I spent half an hour with Thomas Dragovich after his court day ended and he returned to his Grove Street offices. Then, with Dragovich running interference, I spent a few minutes back at the Hall talking to Figone and Samuels, the homicide inspectors working the Daniels investigation, before they went off shift. And then I went back to Bayfront Towers to talk to the evening-shift security people.

There was very little of a positive nature in any of it. None of the four security guards

I spoke with had been working on Saturday and refused to give specific answers to my questions about Verity Daniels's recent activities. "We already told the police everything we know," one of them, George Haxner, said. "You're just wasting your time, anyway. Ms. Daniels told me how your man Runyon tried to rape her. You ask me, he's guilty as hell."

One thing the three East Bay possibles had in common besides apparent animosity toward the dead woman was that they were all in financial difficulty to one degree or another. Ostrander was on the cusp of losing his nursery, like so many other small business owners in this recessive, if not depressive, economy; money borrowed from his brother-in-law, the Danville urologist, was all that was keeping him from a probable Chapter 11. Hank Avery was mired in debt because of his low-paying job and the percentage of his mother's medical bills not covered by Medicare. Canaday's insurance agency was struggling along, but he had a history of taking risky fliers in the stock market and his most recent gamble, just before the market began to nosedive, had resulted in losses he hadn't been able to recoup. It was at least conceivable that one of the three had approached Daniels to beg for a loan, been rebuffed in her typically nasty fashion, and had killed her in retaliation. An angle worth considering, anyway, along with the revenge motive.

Dragovich was candid: unless the police turned up evidence to cast doubt on their case against Runyon, it was unlikely that he'd be able to get the judge at Jake's preliminary hearing to grant bail. And even if he could, the amount would be well up in six figures — prohibitively high even with Abe Melikian as the bondsman. Melikian would be forced to ask for the kind of collateral neither Runyon nor Tamara and I were in a position to supply. So Jake would be bound over for trial, and if it came down to that, his chances were as thin as the threads that had bound that button to the sleeve of his suit coat.

Figone and Samuels seemed open-minded, even willing to lean a little in favor Runyon's innocence — no cop likes to see a former brother officer, particularly one with a record as clean as Jake's, go down for a major crime. They had no objection to my conducting an investigation of my own, as long as I didn't step on their toes and agreed to immediately let them know of anything relevant that I might uncover. But they weren't too sanguine about my chances. Their investigation thus far, which included searches of Runyon's apartment and car, had turned up no additional evidence against him, but they'd also found nothing to refute what they already had: the button; his strength of motive; his lack of an alibi.

The inspectors were willing to share a few details. Verity Daniels had facial contusions and had also been struck with an unidentified object that caused blunt force trauma to her skull. The blow hadn't been fatal; strangulation was the official cause of death. The body had been stripped of clothing, and of the platinum gold wristwatch and blood-ruby ring Runyon had described and any other jewelry she might have been wearing, then wrapped in a sheet of plastic — the common kind painters use as dropcloths — and bound with duct tape. Daniels's BMW had been found in a parking area on Lake Merced Boulevard, on the opposite side of the lake from where her body had been dumped. No signs of violence inside or out, no fingerprints other than hers, no clues of any kind. Figone obliged when I asked for the exact discovery location of the body; that was the only other piece of information I got from them.

I didn't mention Ostrander, Canaday, and

Hank Avery. Premature. I had no reason to believe any of the three was guilty, and cops don't appreciate private citizens trying to influence or muddy up their investigations. Besides which, Figone and Samuels had requested a copy of Runyon's report on the alleged extortion. The three names were right there; it was their business, at least for the time being, whether or not they followed up on any of them.

On my way home from the second futile trip to Bayfront Towers, I took a long detour over to Lake Merced. No particular reason, but it wasn't curiosity, either. The more detailed knowledge you have, the better you're able to do your job.

The lake, big and spring-fed, is in the southwestern corner of the city near the Daly City line. Six-hundred-and-fifty surface acres surrounded by a narrow fringe of parkland and bounded by three golf courses, residential areas, S.F. State University, Fort Funston, and the ocean to the west. SFPD's firearms range is located there, as is a skeet shooting club and a sports center and boat house, and the National Guard Armory is close by. You can fish in it, row or canoe on it, drive or walk or bicycle around it. Off John Muir Drive at the southern end, where it narrows into the area known as Impound

Lake, there's a small parking lot and a concrete footbridge that connects with the opposite shore, and not much else. Tule grass and other vegetation hug the shoreline along there. That was where Verity Daniels had been found, down among the tules at the edge of the lot near the bridge.

I parked near the approximate spot, walked over for a closer look. This area is pretty much deserted late at night, and when heavy fogbanks roll in off the Pacific, as they had on Saturday night, visibility gets cut down toward zero. Easy enough for Daniels's murderer to have driven her BMW in here, cut his lights, hauled the body out, and dumped it over a low pipe-rail fence into the tules. Even if another car had passed by during that time, the driver wouldn't have been able to see anything through the fog. Two minutes, three at the most —

No, more than that. He'd have wanted to make certain Jake's coat button stayed clenched in her hand, didn't somehow get lost in the lake; that was why he'd wrapped the body in the plastic sheeting. He'd have lowered rather than dropped her into the tules so there'd be less chance of the plastic coming loose.

The logistics told me a couple of other

things. First, the perp had wanted the body found and found quickly; joggers, walkers, fishermen were all over this section of the lake in the morning hours. And second, he knew the area. This was not the kind of place you'd pick at random to either commit murder or dispose of a corpse after murder had been done. Did any of the East Bay suspects know Lake Merced that well? Maybe have lived in the city at one time? Something for Tamara to check on.

I drove around the lake and up Lake Merced Boulevard past where Daniels's BMW had been abandoned. There wasn't much along there except the golf club on one side and the lake and parkland on the other — a section that also would have been deserted late on a foggy night. The location raised questions, the same ones that would occur to Figone and Samuels. Had the perp driven the BMW here after dumping the body? Or had he used his own vehicle, then switched it for the BMW at some other place? In that case, what was his reason or reasons for choosing this particular spot? One possibility was that he'd needed a way out of the area and it was easy walking distance to public transportation on 19th Avenue. Unless he'd had an accomplice who'd followed him and picked him up. . . .

Speculating again, giving too much free rein to my imagination. Wasted effort without more facts.

I went on home to Kerry and Emily.

Tuesday.

Runyon's arraignment was scheduled for this morning, but I didn't see any purpose in attending. The police investigation hadn't turned up anything new or I'd have been informed, so it seemed probable that Jake would be bound over for trial. My time could be put to better use in the East Bay.

Martinez first, by way of Highway 80 to Hercules and then Highway 4 across the Briones hills. Coming in from that direction put me closer to the Avery house than downtown, so I made that my first stop. Hank Avery would probably be at work, and it seemed like a good idea to talk to his mother first, if possible, before I saw him. Sometimes you can get useful information by taking a roundabout route through a family member.

At first nobody answered the door at the Avery tract house. But somebody was home: I could hear the television going, bursts of canned hilarity from a sitcom's laugh track. I leaned on the bell, one of those loud buzzer types that overrode the TV noise so the occupant couldn't help but hear it. It took a good three minutes before I finally got a response.

The woman who glared at me through a locked screen door was stick-thin inside an old quilted bathrobe, her uncombed hair frizzed up in tufts and tangles like weeds growing on a fissured, egg-shaped rock. She may have been sick, but aside from the thinness and the facial fissures, she didn't look it. Good color, bright eyes smoky with anger.

"What's the idea ringing my bell like that? What you want?"

"A few minutes of your time, Mrs. Avery. I —"

"Can't you read? No solicitors!" She started to close the door.

I said, "It's about Verity Daniels."

That stopped her in mid-swing. "Who're you?"

"Private investigator." I showed her my credentials, and got a scowl in return.

"You the same one that was here before, talked to my son?"

"No. Same agency, though."

"I got nothing to say to you about that woman Hank didn't tell the other detective."

"The situation's different now."

"Different? What you mean, different?"

"Don't you know? It's been in the news."

"I don't pay no attention to the news. What're you talking about?"

"Verity Daniels is dead. Killed Saturday night."

She stood stock still for maybe ten seconds. Then the scowl melted away and her mouth reshaped into a hangman's smile. "Dead. Now that is news worth having. What happened to her?"

"Could we talk inside, Mrs. Avery? Be easier than through this screen door."

She hesitated, running her tongue around the edges of that dark smile. "Guess it'll be all right," she said, and unlocked the screen.

I followed her slow-shuffling form into a musty-smelling living room filled with mismatched furniture, all of it inexpensive except for what looked to be a new flat-screen television set. Priority item for the masses, price and sacrifice no object. She went to the TV but she didn't switch it off, just lowered the sound.

"Well? How'd she die?"

"She was murdered."

Blink. The smile sagged a little, not much. "Murdered how?"

"Beaten and then strangled."

Helen Avery's mouth shaped the word

Good, but she didn't give voice to it. Instead she said, "Who done it? One of her new rich friends? All that money she inherited . . . you know about that, I guess."

"I know about it," I said. "The police have a suspect in custody, but I don't think he's guilty."

"No? Who is?"

"That's what I'm trying to find out."

All at once she seemed a little shaky on her feet. She sat down in an old recliner next to a table dominated by medicine vials, draped a knitted afghan over her lap, and squinted at an old ticking clock set among the vials. "Time for more of my medicine," she said. I watched her swallow one of the pills with half a glass of water. "I been sick. Real sick for a while, thought I was gonna die. Better now. The doctors say I still have a ways to go, but I'll make it now that I got my Medicare. If Obama don't take it away with his goddamn socialist health-care crap."

I had nothing to say to that. Nothing she'd have wanted to hear, anyway.

She took another sip of water, and the hangman's smile brightened again. "So that woman finally got what was coming to her. Good riddance to bad rubbish, that's what I say, after what she done to my boy Jason.

I guess you know about that, too?"

"I know your son drowned and Verity Daniels was exonerated of any wrongdoing. An unfortunate accident."

"Accident!" Helen Avery spat the word.

"You don't believe it was?"

"No proof it wasn't, that's what the cops told us. No sign of violence on poor Jason's body, and her not strong enough to hold him under water if he was conscious. Well, maybe not. But one way or another she was the cause of him drowning. He'd still be alive if he hadn't got mixed up with that tramp."

"Why was she a tramp?"

"Why do you think? Cheating on Jason the whole time she was engaged to him, just like she cheated on her husband before."

"Facts? Or are you just guessing?"

"Facts, mister."

"How do you know?"

"My other boy, Hank, he found out after what happened to Jason. Tramp's ex told him that was what busted up their marriage, her sleeping around."

"Hank talked to Scott Ostrander? Why?"

"Try to get something on her that'd make the cops change their minds. Well, he found out plenty, not that it done any good. Still the same lying bitch when she was engaged to Jason, sleeping with another man the whole damn time."

"What other man?"

"The one she worked for. And him married with a kid."

"Vincent Canaday?"

Emphatic bob of the frizzy head. "Jason knew it, too. Wouldn't say nothing to us except she was a liar and a cheat, but he must've found out and that's why he wasn't gonna marry her."

"How did Hank find out about her and Canaday?"

"Followed her, saw them together at some motel in Antioch."

"Why was he following her?"

"I told you, prove what a lying bitch she was. We was both so upset about Jason and the way the cops let her off scot-free, he just had to do something."

"Did he confront her about the affair?"

"Sure he did. Walked right up to her and threw it in her face. She didn't turn a hair. Denied it, lied her head off."

"What did Hank do then?"

"Told the cops about her shacking up with her boss." Persimmon mouth, pinched tight at the corners. "Didn't do any good. They said so what, that's her private business, didn't have nothing to do with Jason drowning. Like hell it didn't."

"Did Hank talk to Canaday?"

"No," Helen Avery said. "He wanted to, maybe tell the man's wife what was going on, but I said no, wasn't no purpose in making them kind of waves."

"He keep on following Verity Daniels?"

"No. Wasn't no more reason to. That was when I got sick and couldn't work anymore, and Hank, he had to start working overtime to pay the bills."

"So neither of you had anything more to do with her."

"That's right. Washed her out of our lives until that other detective come around and told Hank about all that money she got."

"That must have been a shock," I said.

"Better believe it was. Us just squeaking by and her living over there in the city in the lap of luxury."

"Made you both hate her even more."

"Well? Wouldn't you?"

"Enough to do something about it?"

Helen Avery was slow on the uptake, but she finally caught on to where I was leading the conversation. Her eyes heated up again into a wrathful glare. "You trying to say Hank had something to do with her being murdered?" she snapped.

"I'm not accusing him —"

"He wouldn't hurt nobody, not even her. You hear me? Not my Hank!"

"Then you won't mind telling me where he was on Saturday."

"Right here, right here with me!"

"All day, all night?"

She struggled onto her feet, stood swaying and glaring; the finger she aimed at me was like the barrel of a pistol. "You get out of here! You get out of my house right now or I'll call the cops on you! *Get out!*"

I got out.

With plenty to think about as I drove away. The affair between Verity Daniels and Vincent Canaday that had been going on at the time of her engagement to Jason Avery . . . and how long since? Hank Avery's stalking of Daniels two years ago. The connection between him and Scott Ostrander. Helen Avery's rush to alibi her son for Saturday. None of it conclusive, or necessarily incriminating, but all of it worth following up on.

18

Vincent Canaday was not in his office at Gateway Insurance. One of the two women employees told me he had "business in San Francisco" that morning and expected to return by one o'clock. Could she help me? Or did I want to leave a message for Mr. Canaday? I said no to both questions, that I'd check back early afternoon. Better to brace him cold.

Scott Ostrander was next on my list. But when I got to Ostrander's Nursery and Landscaping Service, the front gate was locked and bore a CLOSED sign. There were no posted hours, but it seemed unusual that a struggling business wouldn't be open at eleven on a weekday morning. Unless the Ostranders' financial troubles had slid beyond the struggling point and the nursery had been shut down by them or their creditors. I went to two of the neighboring businesses to see what I could find out. Not much. None of the people I talked to knew why the nursery was closed; it had been open on Saturday and was normally open every day except Sunday.

The Ostranders lived in a modest Orinda neighborhood of small tract houses maybe twenty years old. The property was well landscaped in rock-garden style, though there were indications that the plantings and flagstone walkways hadn't received much attention recently. The driveway and curb in front were empty. So was the house, evidently; at least nobody responded to my ring.

Now what?

Too soon to head back for Martinez and Gateway Insurance, unless I stopped somewhere for lunch first. But I wasn't hungry; my appetite had slacked off considerably since July, and I was pretty much down to two meals a day — a light breakfast and a modest dinner.

Scott Ostrander's sister, then. Danville was only about fifteen miles south of Orinda, off Highway 680. According to the information Tamara had gleaned, Grace Lyman had no job or profession and her primary activity seemed to be helping to organize community activities. Maybe she'd be home and willing to answer some questions.

Danville is the most affluent of the Contra Costa communities, home to the exclusive gated Blackhawk community, which is in turn home to a world-famous classic car museum, an upscale shopping plaza, and a passel of local celebrities of one stripe and another. The Lymans didn't live in Blackhawk, but their home in the rolling countryside wasn't far removed from it — a big, older California ranch-style place, probably custom built, fronted by an artistic arrangement of small trees and shrubs and garden statuary. More of Scott Ostrander's capable work, I thought.

On a curving driveway inside a pair of ornamental pillars, a lime green Mercedes sat in front of a two-car garage. So somebody was here. Fortunately it turned out to be Grace Lyman, a willowy blonde in her late thirties aging well without the aid of plastic surgery or Botox or collagen injections; the tiny lines around her eyes and mouth enhanced rather than detracted from her good looks. Nice eyes, too, the kind of blue-green color that changes subtly with different moods, different lighting.

She was reluctant to talk to me at first. Guarded, leery of my intentions and protective of her brother. She knew Verity Daniels had been murdered from an Internet news report she'd read yesterday, and seemed to think I might be trying to involve him in the crime. I did some fast talking, managed to convince her that I had no preconceived notions and my only interest was in proving my associate innocent. Now and then there's an advantage to being a business-man of my age: younger people tend to look at me, when they look at me at all, as grandfatherly and nonthreatening.

Even so, Grace Lyman didn't seem to want me inside her house. She said, "All right, but I can only give you a few minutes — I have company coming for lunch at one. We can talk on the terrace in back. Just fol-low that path there. I'll join you shortly."

The path led around the side, through more plantings, and emerged into a large area dominated by a swimming pool with a rock waterfall at one end. A flagstone ter-race stretched out between the house and the pool, white wrought-iron furniture ar-ranged on it under striped umbrellas. One of the pair of tables held four place settings on woven mats. I stood behind a chair at the second, empty table to wait.

Pretty soon Mrs. Lyman came out carry-ing a towel-wrapped bottle of wine inside a silver ice bucket. She put that down on the place-set table before she invited me to occupy the chair at the other one.

"Did you talk to Scott before you came here?" she asked when we were both seated.

"As a matter of fact, no. His nursery is closed today and there's no one at his home."

"Yes, well, he and his wife had a . . . business appointment today."

The way she said it told me the appointment was related to the Ostranders' financial troubles, so I didn't press her. Instead I asked, "Does he know his ex-wife is dead?"

"Yes. I called and told him when I found out."

"How did he take the news?"

"Well, he wasn't happy about it, any more than I was. Murder is a horrible crime. But I won't pretend either of us is sorry Verity Daniels is gone. She had a ruinous effect on Scott's life."

"How do you mean, ruinous?"

I watched Mrs. Lyman consider whether or not to answer. Finally, "I don't like to speak ill of the dead, but . . . How much do you know about her?"

"A fair amount, but it would help to know more."

"Well . . . she was a dreadful woman. My

husband believes she was mentally ill and I have no doubt he's right. A shrew and a compulsive liar . . . my God, the lies she told, the stories she made up. She was incapable of telling the truth about anything."

"What sort of stories?"

Emotions played across Grace Lyman's face — memory shadows, I thought. Her antipathy toward Verity Daniels must have been pretty intense; it melted some of her reticence, opened her up in spite of herself.

"Ridiculous fantasies," she said. "Conspiracies against her, conspiracies in her workplace. Men following her, trying to attack her. Obscene phone callers. Neighbors spying on her while she was naked in the shower. Most of it came from television — she watched TV incessantly when she wasn't working or playing her silly games or out buying things she and Scott didn't need and couldn't afford. Or sneaking around behind his back. She always had to be the center of attention, always had to feed her sick craving for excitement. Scott put up with it for two years before the final straw. But by then he was in debt, and except for his second marriage to Karen, a *good* marriage, nothing has gone right for him since."

"What was the final straw?"

"I'm not sure Scott would want me to discuss that."

"I may already know the answer," I said. "He found out she was seeing another man."

Nothing for five or six beats. Then, "I'm sorry, but I dislike euphemisms. Not seeing another man, she was *fucking* another man. The whole time Scott was married to her. She admitted it when he finally caught on."

"How did he catch on?"

"He stumbled across a box Verity had hidden in her closet. Money, some expensive pieces of jewelry he hadn't given her" — Mrs. Lyman's mouth curled distastefully — "and a couple of those graphic notes illicit lovers write to each other. At first she tried to pretend she'd saved the money, bought the jewelry, and written the notes herself. But Scott kept pressing her until she lost control and screamed the truth at him. She had a really vicious temper when she was provoked."

"Did she name the man?"

"Oh, yes. Her boss at the insurance agency where she worked."

"Vincent Canaday," I said, thinking: So her affair with Canaday stretched all the way back to the time of her marriage to Scott Ostrander. Five years, at least. Ongoing? On again, off again? Pretty serious relationship, in any case.

"Yes, Vincent Canaday," Mrs. Lyman said. "Of all people, after what she once said about him."

"How do you mean?"

"One of her fantasies. The workplace conspiracy I mentioned."

"What sort of conspiracy?"

Just then a fat blue jay came swooping down out of one of the pines that rimmed the yard, landed on the place-set table, and sat there screeching like a banshee. Grace Lyman came out of her chair so quickly she might have been ejected, chased the bird off by yelling and flapping her arms. It flew back into the tree and kept right on screeching.

"Jays," she said when she came back, as if it were an obscene word. "I can't stand those birds, they drive me to distraction sometimes."

"Pretty noisy," I agreed.

She sat down again. "What was it you asked me?"

"You were going to tell me about Verity Daniels's workplace conspiracy."

"Oh, that. I don't remember exactly . . . some nonsense about defrauding one of the insurance companies the agency represented."

"And it was Canaday who was doing the defrauding?"

"So she claimed. When she found out about it he tried to enlist her help, but she refused. She talked him into returning the money, and he gave her a raise so she'd never tell anybody what he'd done. Some silliness like that."

"She didn't say exactly what the alleged fraud was?"

"If she did, Scott didn't tell me."

"Or how much money was involved?"

"No. What does it matter? It was just another of her games."

Maybe. And maybe not.

I asked, "When did she make this claim, do you recall?"

"No, I . . . wait, yes I do. It was around Christmas, the year before she admitted to the affair. Scott asked her where she'd gotten the money to buy something or other and she said it was from a raise in her salary. Then she told him the fraud story."

"About the affair. How long had it been going on?"

"A long time. She didn't provide exact dates."

Two years is a long time. So is one year. Pre-fraud or post-fraud, assuming there was any truth to the story? If there was, and the affair had begun post-fraud, it opened up the possibility that Daniels had blackmailed Canaday into it and kept him on the hook for a long time afterward. And blackmail, if the pigeon decides he's had enough, is a strong motive for murder.

I asked, "Did your brother name Canaday when he filed for divorce?"

"No. He could have . . . should have, given the demands she made. Alimony, for God's sake, when she was making almost as much money as Scott. If they'd owned rather than rented their home, she'd have tried to force him to sell it. As it was, he gave her a larger share of their community property just to be free of her."

"Has your brother had any contact with her since the divorce?"

"Of course not. Why should he, after what she put him through?"

I waited a couple of seconds before I said, "I understand he was pretty upset when he found out about her inheritance."

"Well? Wouldn't you be if you were him?"

"Probably."

"He didn't do anything about it, if that's what you're thinking," Grace Lyman said.

"But he is in serious need of money."

That bought me a sharp look. "What are

you suggesting? That he went to her and begged for a loan? Scott would sooner have cut off his hand. Don't you understand? She was a blight on his life, a plague to him. He'd never have had anything to do with her, not for *any* reason."

I said mildly, "Hate is a pretty strong emotion."

"Yes, it is. But my brother is a passive person, completely nonviolent. If he'd wanted to . . . hurt Verity, if he'd been capable of so much as slapping her, he'd have done it when she threw her affair in his face."

I let that pass without comment.

"The kind of woman she was, dozens of people probably had cause to kill her. Vincent Canaday, for one. Why aren't you investigating him?"

"I am," I said. "Hank Avery, too, among others."

"Who?"

"Hank Avery, the brother of the man Verity Daniels was engaged to three years ago."

"Oh, yes, the man who was drowned in the Delta."

"You know about the incident, then."

"Scott told me. I think he said the man's brother came to see him, that's how he found out. Verity was absolved of any wrongdoing, but the man didn't believe it. Hank Avery, yes. He knew about Verity's affair with Canaday, too. He and Scott talked about it."

"Do you know if your brother's seen Avery since?"

"I doubt that he has. He'd have no reason to." The jay was still shrieking; Grace Lyman glared in the bird's direction, then looked at her watch. "My God, it's twelve-thirty. You'll have to leave now. My guests will be arriving soon and I still have things to do in the kitchen."

I didn't argue, just got to my feet and thanked her for her time and for being frank with me.

She was already regretting it; the way her changeable eyes had darkened told me that. She said, "I suppose you're going to see Scott anyway."

"I won't tell him about our conversation, if you'd rather I didn't."

"That doesn't matter, we have no secrets from each other. But is it really necessary to bother him? He has enough to deal with as it is. Have some compassion, can't you?"

"I do, for anybody in trouble. Especially a friend and associate who's been accused of crimes he didn't commit. If your brother is innocent of any wrongdoing, he has nothing to fear from me."

"He'd better not have."

Exit line: she walked away quickly toward the house. But she didn't go inside while I was still in her sight, and maybe not until after she heard my car start up out front.

19

On the way out of Danville I spotted a Taco Bell and turned into the parking lot. Not to eat — junk food is not one of my vices — but to buy a cup of bad coffee and make some phone calls.

The first call was to the agency to check in with Tamara. She'd gone to Runyon's arraignment — moral support — and I asked her how it had gone.

"As we expected," she said bleakly. "Nothing new on the police investigation, and the hotshot from the DA's office argued that there was enough evidence to bind Jake over for trial. Judge agreed."

"Without bail?"

"Yeah. Hard-ass, that judge. Dragovich tried to get him to set a reasonable figure, but he said the assault charge combined with the murder charge established what he called 'a pattern of behavior' that made Jake a potential danger to society. Bail denied.

So it's up to us to get him the hell out before the trial."

"Judge set a trial date?"

"Not yet. Just scheduled a consultation with Dragovich and the ADA to determine when it'll be. Dragovich says at least three months, probably longer on account of the jammed-up court calendar."

"Well, that gives us plenty of time, at least."

"Longer it takes us, the longer Jake sits in a damn cell."

"Try not to think about that," I said. But it was spurious advice; I was thinking about it myself. "You have a chance to check on whether any of the possible suspects in Daniels's past lived in the city?"

"Yeah, Canaday did. For a couple of years when he was working for Pacific Rim Insurance."

"When was that?"

"Ten years ago."

Long time — too long to remember Lake Merced? "Any of the three have relatives in the city?"

"Nope. Nor any friends or business associates I could locate. You find out anything so far?"

"Some things we didn't know about." I filled her in on the information I'd gathered from Helen Avery and Grace Lyman.

"Makes Avery and Canaday look like our best bets," Tamara said. "Avery stalked Daniels once, maybe he started doing it again."

"For what reason?"

"Pissed off about all the money she inherited. Got a mad on, stalked her, caught her alone somewhere and got up in her face, she went off on him, he lost it and killed her."

"That would make sense if it'd happened two and a half years ago. He didn't resort to violence then, it's not likely he'd do it now. At least not for revenge. There'd have to be another reason for him to be guilty."

"Money. Maybe he thought he could get some out of her."

"Possible but not likely," I said.

"Well, then, there's Canaday. He needs money badly, too."

"So he does." And if he had gone to Daniels for a handout, that blew off the remote possibility of her having blackmailed him into their affair. Blackmailers don't loan money to their victims. "How heavy were his recent losses?"

"Pretty heavy, from what I can find out."

"Recoup at any time? Pay off any of his debts?"

"Doesn't look like it," Tamara said. "Could be he tried borrowing from Daniels when she collected her two million and she turned him down. Or only gave him enough to dig himself a deeper hole. So he went back for more, she blew him off, there was a fight and she ended up dead."

"Viable scenario if he was still involved with her before and after she inherited. Make that if he was involved with her in the first place."

"Why if? Daniels admitted they were getting it on, right? And everybody you talked to confirmed it."

"Daniels was a liar — her confession to Ostrander could've been a lie, too. The rest is all hearsay so far. What Avery told his mother, what Ostrander told his sister."

"One way to verify it."

"Ask Canaday," I said. "I intend to, though probably not straight out. How long has he been playing the market and losing? Back as far as five years?"

"Longer. Two mortgages on his home, a personal loan that he's close to defaulting on."

"Always in need of money, then. Badly strapped at times."

"Yep. You thinking maybe there's something to Daniels's workplace fraud story?"

"Keeping an open mind. It wouldn't be anything Canaday could get away with long term, but there are ways for a risk-taker with his own agency to get his hands on cash for short periods. Phony claims. Convincing customers to make out premium checks to him instead of to the insurance company. You have a list of the companies he brokers for?"

"No, but I can get one."

"Do that, and then check with the companies. Use some ploy to find out if any of them have had reason to question Canaday's business practices."

"Leave it to me, boss."

The coffee was cold now, wouldn't have been worth finishing even if it weren't. I got out of the car to dump it, got back in, and called home to find out how Kerry was getting on.

But I didn't find out.

Eight, nine, ten rings — no answer.

Didn't necessarily mean anything. She might have been so deeply involved in one of her advertising projects that she ignored the phone. Or in the bathroom. Or taking a nap; she wasn't sleeping as much now as she had been for a while, but when she did nap she tended to sleep deeply. But the non-response tightened my nerves just the same.

As if I didn't have enough to worry about.

Call number three went to Gateway Insurance, to determine if Vincent Canaday had returned yet. Good thing I called instead of driving all the way back to Martinez; he not only hadn't come back, he wasn't going to. The woman I spoke to told me he'd called in a few minutes ago to say that he was "coming down with something" and was going straight home. "He really didn't sound well at all," she said.

One more call to my home.

Still no answer.

Vincent Canaday lived in Lafayette, a former Mexican land grant that had evolved into another of the moneyed communities strung out along and among the tree-studded hills north of Danville. The GPS I'd reluctantly installed some time back, but had come to rely on, led me on a twisty upward path southwest of downtown and finally onto a street of large homes on woodsy lots.

Canaday's place was a kind of bastardized Spanish style, all jutting angles and rounded corners, set back behind a six-foot-high, tile-topped wall and fronted by a tall heritage oak. There were two entrances, one for vehicles and the other for walk-ins, both made of arched wood set into wall pillars so that you couldn't see inside from the street. The main entrance gate wasn't locked; I opened it, stepped into a tiled patio. The oak stood in the middle of it, encircled by a low stucco wall, and there were yucca trees and cactus and some other plants along the house walls. At one time the patio area must have been pretty nice; not so much now. Some of the tiles were cracked, with weeds growing up through them, and the plantings had a neglected look. When people like Canaday are short on money, gardeners are among the first to be let go.

The steps leading up to the front door were of stucco inlaid with bits and pieces of multicolored tile. The bottom step had a jagged crack running through it and some of the tiles there were missing. I went up and thumbed the bell, waited, thumbed it again, waited, leaned on it a third time. Nobody came to open either the door or its squared-off, gated peephole.

If Canaday was home, he wasn't dealing with visitors.

In the car I called home again. And this time, to my considerable relief, Kerry answered on the third ring.

"I tried to get you a couple of times

earlier," I said. "Were you busy, or — ?"

"Checking up on me?"

"No, no . . ."

"Yes, you were." But she didn't sound upset about it. "I wasn't here when you called. I went out for a walk."

"A walk?" I said, surprised. "By yourself?"

"Well, there's nobody else here. Yes, by myself."

"Where'd you go?"

"Not far. Up and down the block. I decided it was time . . . past time I stopped hiding like an animal in a cave and started putting my life back together."

"Good. Good!" It was all I could think of to say.

"Going out alone was easier than I thought it would be," she said. "I'm not going to rush it, but . . . I'll be myself again eventually. I mean that."

"I never doubted it."

"Just do me one favor, will you?"

"Name it."

"No more calls to check up. I'll do what I have to do, you do what you have to do. Like before. Like always with us."

"Like always," I agreed.

Orinda is Lafayette's immediate neighbor to the north, Walnut Creek its immediate neighbor on the south. Two choices, then: another swing by Ostrander's Nursery and Landscaping, or a visit to Riteway Gutter Installers. I wanted a conversation with Hank Avery, but I don't like bracing a potentially hostile individual in his workplace; and Avery would be hostile for sure if he'd talked to his mother since my visit this morning. Besides, his work as an installer likely meant he'd be out somewhere on a job. So I opted for Orinda, mainly to kill time until Avery's workday ended; I didn't expect the nursery to be open.

But it was, the gates standing wide. And both Ostranders were there, inside a cubbyhole office going over some papers spread out on a desk. If the bleak look of them was any indication, the "business appointment" they'd had earlier today had not gone well.

Ostrander's first response when I showed him my credentials and told him why I was there: "Can't you people leave me alone? I don't know anything about Verity's murder — I don't want to know anything about it."

"I didn't say that you did."

"Then why come to me? She got what she deserved, that's all I have to say."

"Your sister said the same thing."

"Grace? You been bothering her, too?"

"Information, Mr. Ostrander. I'll talk to

247

anyone I have to to get it. She told me some things I'd like clarified."

"What things?"

"For one, your relationship with Hank Avery."

Ostrander frowned, scrubbed a hand through sparse sandy hair. "Who the hell is Hank Avery?"

I refreshed his memory. "When did you last see him?"

"I only saw him that one time he showed up to tell me what I already knew."

"He seem surprised that you knew? Or that the affair had been going on as long as it had?"

"No. He knew as well as I did what she was."

"And hated her for what he believed she'd done to his brother."

"Had cause, didn't he?"

"What do you think of the notion that your ex-wife was responsible for Jason Avery's death?"

"Sure she was responsible. One way or another."

"Does that mean you think she might have been responsible for him drowning? Was she capable of a thing like that?"

"She was capable of anything if she wanted it badly enough."

"Doesn't quite answer my question. There's some evidence to indicate she was given to violent outbursts. Would you agree?"

"Hell, yes," Ostrander said. "Mainly she'd just cut you up with her lies, but if she got mad enough, didn't get her way, she could be a hellcat."

"Did you tell that to Hank Avery?"

"I might have. I don't remember."

"How about him? He strike you as the violent type?"

"Acted tough, said he'd like to see her get hers, but she was still walking around two years later. Maybe something set him off again, I don't know. Why don't you go ask him?"

"I will."

"And that man she was sleeping with all those years." This from Karen Ostrander, who'd been standing close to her husband and frowning at me the entire time we'd been talking. "He might have had reason to want her dead."

"He's on my list," I said. Then, to Ostrander, "Do you know Vincent Canaday?"

"No."

"Never had any dealings with him?"

"Never even met him. No reason to before I found out he was screwing Verity, sure as hell none afterward."

"Except maybe to accuse him."

"I didn't want anything to do with him. Or her. Still don't. Are we done here now? I have work to do."

"One more question. Where were you Saturday evening?"

His mouth quirked sardonically. "Is that when Verity was killed?"

"Yes."

"Well, that's just dandy. I was on a landscaping job until six that afternoon, and home from six-thirty on. Karen will vouch for that. So will two of our neighbors who came over around eight to play cards and stayed until eleven. You want their names?"

"No. Not necessary."

"So you'll leave us alone from now on?" his wife asked.

I said, "You won't see me again," and meant it.

Scratch Scott Ostrander off the list of possibles.

20

I'd asked Ostrander if Hank Avery was the violent type. I had an answer to that sooner than expected, up close and personal.

My timing was good on the return trip to Martinez: I arrived at the Avery home just as a somewhat battered brown pickup was pulling into the driveway. I swung over to the curb in front, climbed out just as the pickup's driver emerged. Barrel-shaped guy with a bushy mustache and an aggressive stance. He watched me through narrowed eyes as I cut across a corner of the weedy lawn to the driveway.

"Hank Avery?"

Now that he'd got a good look at me, his face clouded up and the eyes radiated anger. "You're the guy come around hassling my mother this morning."

"So she told you about our talk. I thought she might."

"You got a lot of balls, coming back." He

took a step toward me, his hands opening and closing by his sternum like a boxer warming up. "Haul your ass outta here and don't come around again."

"There's no need for belligerence, Mr. Avery. I only want a few words with you —"

"I don't want no words with *you*. Fuck off."

"Look, I've got a job to do and I intend to do it whether you like it or not. I don't have anything against you, but if you have nothing to hide —"

"That's right, nothing to hide." Another step, this one close enough so that his chest nearly touched mine and I could smell his breath. Mint over whiskey: he'd had a drink or three somewhere on the way home. I didn't move, matching his unblinking gaze.

"Then you don't have anything to fear from me."

"Fear? From an old fart like you? Jesus Christ! I ain't gonna tell you again. Fuck off."

"Or what? You'll call the police?"

"I don't need no police to deal with assholes."

"Does your mother know you use language like that?"

His face was blood-dark now. He said,

snarling the words, "I don't give a shit if you're old, I had enough of you," and banged the heel of one hand into my chest. Not a tap, a blow hard enough to hurt and to stagger me into a backward two-step shuffle.

Well, it had been a long day and I was tired and in no mood to be forbearing. I didn't mind the old fart, old man stuff too much — by most standards that's just what I am — but I'm neither feeble nor senile and I damn well did mind being punched by a pugnacious stranger. When I regained my balance I came right back at Avery, jabbed both palms into his chest, and shoved with as much force as I could muster. He wasn't expecting retaliation; the shove sent him pinwheeling backward off balance. His upper body thudded into the pickup's door, and when he caromed off, his feet slid out from under him and down he went, hard, on his chunky ass.

He sat there looking stunned for about five seconds. Then he made a snorting noise like an enraged bull, scrambled to his feet, started toward me again.

"I wouldn't," I said.

Something in my voice, my expression, the way I was standing brought him up short. He glared at me, his hands flexing open and closed again. I glared back. Standoffs like this were my meat; I'd been through too many to count or remember. This one lasted for fifteen seconds or so, during which time his aggressiveness gave way to a surly petulance. The old fart had embarrassed him, wounded his thorny male pride — not that he would ever admit it to himself or anyone else. But the fact was, he didn't want anything more to do with me; he wanted to go inside and put salve on his ego-wound by telling Momma how he'd got rid of me.

His parting shot wasn't much, about what I expected: "The hell with it and the hell with you, man. You come around here again, I damn well will call the cops on you."

And he was gone, and thirty seconds later so was I. But not until I noted and wrote down the license plate number of Avery's pickup.

I heard from Tamara while I was still within the Martinez city limits. And as usual, I pulled over to take the call. Most Californians seem defiantly determined to ignore the laws against talking and texting on hand-held cell phones while driving, but I'm not one of them. Laws aren't always good laws for a good reason, but this one was. Tamara, Runyon, and Alex Chavez all had those hands-free Bluetooth devices in their vehicles; so did Kerry, who kept trying to convince me to follow suit. I kept resisting. I can be stubborn sometimes where change is concerned, particularly when it involves technology. For the present, the GPS unit was as far as I was willing to go.

The only problem with pulling over in this instance was that there was a solid line of cars parked along the curb and I had to drive three more blocks before I found a space. The damn phone kept yammering at me, and when I finally got parked and grabbed for it, it slipped out of my hand and clattered onto the floor on the passenger side. I leaned over to reach for it, and it squirted under the seat. It took a couple more fumbling tries to get hold of it and haul it out. I growled a hello.

"Hey," Tamara said, "don't bite my head off."

"Sorry. I dropped the phone. Sometimes these bloody things are more trouble than they're worth."

She let me hear one of her wry little chuckles. "No chance of you ever becoming a nomophobe."

"A what?"

"Nomophobe. People with an irrational

fear of being separated from their cell phones. Some of 'em even sleep with their phones to make sure they don't get lost or misplaced."

My God.

"Anyhow," she said, "I couldn't get much on Canaday's relationship with the insurance companies he represents. You know how close-mouthed they can be about their employees. Same with agency reps. But it's not a dead end yet. We've done business with one of the companies, Western Maritime and Life, and I've got a contact in their personnel department. I talked her into doing some checking for me."

"How soon will she get back to you?"

"Probably not until tomorrow. You get anything out of Canaday?"

"Haven't talked to him yet. He didn't come back to his office, called in and said he was sick. But if he went home, he's not answering his doorbell. What kind of car does he drive, do you know?"

"Let's see . . . Yeah. Chrysler Town and Country, two years old. Tan, four-door."

"License plate number?"

"Personalized. G-W-A-Y-I-N-S. Some kind of lead there?"

"I don't know yet. Maybe."

"Hank Avery. You see him?"

I told her about the minor dustup in his driveway.

"So he's a hot-headed dude," she said.

"He is," I said, "but more smoke than fire. One of those snarling types that show a yellow streak when push comes to shove. Not that that eliminates him. His mother says he was home with her when Daniels was killed, but that kind of alibi isn't worth much."

"Ostrander?"

"He's out," I said, and explained why.

"So we're down to Avery and Canaday. One of 'em better be guilty. Otherwise . . ."

Otherwise we'd have to start over, look elsewhere. And with little or nothing to point the way.

When I came off the Bay Bridge into San Francisco, it was nearly five o'clock. I swung back down to the Embarcadero and into the Bayfront Towers garage. The evening shift security guard, a crewcut blond with stoic features named Frank Krikowski, was the least unsympathetic of the ones I'd spoken to previously, but still reluctant to answer my questions.

"I told you before," he said, "we're not supposed to discuss the residents. Particularly not Ms. Daniels."

"The police instruct you not to talk about her?"

"No, but it's company policy."

"Look, Jake Runyon has worked in law enforcement for more than twenty years. He's a good man, an honest man — I'd stake my life on his innocence. You can bend the rules a little to help me prove it, can't you?"

Krikowski studied me while he thought it over. Then he shrugged and said, "Up to a point, maybe. What do you want to know?"

"If Ms. Daniels had any visitors recently who looked like either of these two men." I described Hank Avery, and Vincent Canaday from Runyon's report.

"The sandy-haired one, maybe," Krikowski said. "But I see a lot of people every day. Most faces don't stick in my memory."

"How about cars?"

"Not unless there's something real distinctive about it."

"Battered brown Ford pickup with a scrape on one side?"

"Uh-uh. I'd remember a junker like that."

"Tan four-door Chrysler Town and Country, two years old?"

"Pretty common model. No."

"I don't suppose you keep a logbook list

of license plates?"

"Not unless there's a reason to," he said. "If a visitor is expected and we have the name, no. If it's a stranger calling unannounced on one of the residents, yes."

"Along with the person's name?"

"That's right."

"Could you check the book for a couple of names and numbers?"

"I suppose so. But why don't you just go up and talk to George Haxner on the lobby desk? All visitors, expected or not, have to sign in before they're admitted upstairs. No exceptions."

"I'll do that. But I'd appreciate your logbook check first. Say for the past month or so."

He checked. Neither Avery's nor Canaday's names and license plate numbers were listed.

I rode the visitors' elevator up to the lobby. George Haxner, dark and bulky, had the stern look of a prison guard at his post behind the security desk. I shared the opinion Runyon had expressed in his report: Bayfront Towers had more of an institutional feel than a place designed for comfortable urban living.

"You again," Haxner said when I approached. "Now what?"

"Couple more questions."

"Questions about what?"

"Whether or not Verity Daniels had visitors named Vincent Canaday or Hank Avery in the past few weeks. And if so, how often."

"Canaday, Avery . . . who're they?"

"Men she used to know, maybe still knew."

"Police never asked about either one."

"They don't know about them yet."

"But you do. Must be some detective."

"Forty years in the business, public and private."

"Almost twenty for me. I'm still not a genius."

I let that pass.

Haxner said, "So why do you want to know if either of them visited Ms. Daniels?"

"If you could just take a look at the records —"

"Can't do it. I like my job too much."

"No one has to know."

"I'd know. You'd know. Maybe the police would find out. Uh-uh, no, sorry. There's nothing I can do to help you."

21

Wednesday was a bust.

Vincent Canaday didn't show up at Gateway Insurance. "I'm sorry, he's not available today," the woman I talked to on the phone said. I told her I'd been in the day before and asked if he was still under the weather. She didn't know, she hadn't spoken to him. She sounded a little nonplussed when she said that, an indication that he hadn't called in nor had she been able to reach him.

Tamara had both his home and cell numbers. A call to the cell got me an out-of-service message and an invitation to leave one of my own on his voice mail, which I ignored. An answering machine picked up at the home number. No message there, either.

Canaday seemed to have gone to ground for some reason. Maybe related to Verity Daniels's murder; the timing seemed to support a connection. But there could be several other explanations, among them that he really was ill. That would account for the fact Nancy Canaday, who had no job or profession outside her home, was also unavailable.

Tamara's contact at Great Western Maritime and Life came through as promised, but with little in the way of definite information. Five years ago, at the time Verity Daniels claimed he was working some sort of insurance scam, Canaday had been the subject of an internal review with regard to a pair of policies he'd written that the company considered to be "of an inappropriate nature." He'd been reprimanded, but that was all: not enough evidence of deliberate wrongdoing for Great Western to terminate their relationship with him and Gateway Insurance. There was nothing in his file to indicate that they'd had any problems with him since.

Those two suspicious policies made me want a face-to-face with him all the more. But he still wasn't answering his cell, and I kept getting the home answering machine each time I tried that number. And there was nothing to be gained in driving over to the East Bay again unless I was sure I had a chance of getting to him. Frustrating.

At one o'clock I left the office to keep an appointment Tamara had made for me with Thomas Dragovich. More frustration. He'd been in touch with Figone and Samuels; the police investigation so far hadn't turned up anything that even slightly weakened the case against Jake Runyon. The only piece of new information had come from the Bayfront Towers security staff. Evidently Verity Daniels had had a habit of leaving early in the morning two or three days a week, at various times from six-thirty to eight o'clock, and returning at noon or early afternoon. She had also gone off for long periods on Saturday and Sunday, though not leaving as early as on weekdays. This had been going on for a couple of months. But nobody had any idea where she went or what she did during those absences.

A police search of her condo had revealed no links to anyone, male or female. Interviews with Bayfront residents had been equally unproductive. Most had never met or even seen her, and of those who had, only one, a man named Chad Weatherford, had exchanged more than a few words with her. Weatherford had admitted to meeting her in the basement garage one afternoon, sharing an elevator ride with her, and suggesting they have dinner together. She'd turned him down, claiming she was engaged to be married.

I said, "This Weatherford — who is he?"

"CEO of a local software company," Dragovich said.

"Married?"

"No."

"Know anything else about him?"

"No, but there's no reason not to believe his story. He volunteered the information about the dinner date turndown. I don't think we need to concern ourselves with him."

When I got back to the agency, Tamara had a small piece of news for me. "Well, now we know why Canaday's wife hasn't been around to answer their home phone."

"Oh? Why?"

"Doesn't live there anymore. Left him and filed for divorce a little over a month ago. Took their daughter with her, moved in with a sister in San Jose."

"How did you find this out?"

Tamara let me see one of her sly little smiles. "Got my ways."

The Internet, of course. The modern equivalent of Orwell's Big Brother, with the only difference being that anybody can access the vast storehouses of accumulated information. There's no privacy anymore, nothing sacred, no intimate details that can't be ferreted out through one source or another. It's a boon to our profession, sure, making detective work a lot easier than it used to be, but at times it makes me a little nervous about the future. And I find myself thinking of a Fredric Brown vignette I'd read once, in which all the cybernetic machines on all the populated planets in the universe are linked together to form a single super computer. The first question it's asked is the age-old one: Is there a God? And the super computer answers: Yes, *now* there is. . . .

"Hey," Tamara said, "you just go into brainlock or something?"

"Senior moment." I shook off the gloomy reflection, refocused. "What prompted Canaday's wife to walk out?"

"She's not talking, but it's gotta be money problems. Honey problems, too, I bet."

"Other women?"

"Dude's like most men — never pass up an opportunity to have their knobs turned by somebody new. The marriage almost busted up once seven years ago over a woman. Not Verity Daniels, so she wasn't his first and only."

Knobs turned. Right. Join forces with a streetwise twentysomething, get a liberal education in modern slanguage.

"Who was the woman seven years ago?"

"Nobody for us to bother with. Worked in an office near Gateway Insurance, came from Chicago and moved back there after the affair busted up."

"Lengthy affair?"

"Few months. Not anywhere near as long as the one with Daniels."

"So she must have been a lot more to Canaday than a bed partner. Daniels, I mean."

"Probably did some kinky stuff between the sheets that kept him coming back," Tamara said. "She was the type for sex games along with all the other ones she played."

"Either that, or the relationship went beyond the physical."

"For him, maybe. Not for a head case like her."

"She had to be getting something out of it."

"Besides orgasms? Big thrill because he was married and she could keep him dangling. Liar, manipulator, control freak."

Despite Dragovich's comment that we needn't concern ourselves with Chad Weatherford, I asked Tamara to run a backgrounder on him. Transplanted San Franciscan, forty years old, single for the past ten years after a brief marriage. Considered one of the best men in his field of specialized software design; annual income upward of $500,000. Something of a swinger, his name romantically linked with a couple of women among the city's elite. No criminal record of any kind. Just your average rich, handsome, man-on-the-prowl-about-town — the type that considers all women fair game and hits on any reasonably attractive female he meets. Verity Daniels's turndown probably hadn't bothered him in the slightest; for every woman who said no, there'd be several who said yes.

"I can't stand guys like that," Tamara said. "Think they're God's gift. Only thing they care about is their own dick."

"You're too young to be so cynical, kiddo."

"With my track record with men? Uh-uh." For a few seconds she was broodingly silent. Then she muttered, "Damn that man!"

"Who? Weatherford?"

"Horace."

"That's a name I haven't heard you mention in a while."

"Thought I was done with him," she said. "Why the hell couldn't he just stay in Philadelphia?"

"You mean he's back here?"

"Coming back, yeah. Called me up out of the blue last week. Lost his chair at the philharmonic, marriage busted up, got no place else to go. Better believe he's gonna try to mess with my life again."

"Not if you don't let him."

"Easier said than done. You don't know the man like I do."

No, I didn't. But there was one thing I did know, not that I'd invite her anger by saying so: in spite of how much Horace had hurt her, she was still in love with him.

After dinner that evening, I sat tilted back in my recliner and read through the Verity Daniels case file again. Runyon's report, Tamara's various notes, the additions I'd made. Good time for study and reflection because it was quiet in the condo, Kerry working in her office, Emily closeted in her room with schoolwork, iPod, and Shameless the cat.

I didn't really expect to find anything I'd missed previously, and I didn't: all the facts were there, considered and acted upon. And yet when I was done I had one of those nagging feelings that I was overlooking something about Verity Daniels and that nasty, calculated flimflam of hers . . . something in Runyon's detailed report. I read the report again, still couldn't tell what it was. And again — and then I had it.

Baker Beach.

Lands End.

Why had Daniels picked those places for the two bogus rendezvous? Personal experience? She'd lived in the city long enough to have become familiar with both, except that she hadn't been the type to go exploring; couch potato, TV junkie. Selected at random, then, off a map of the city or out of a guidebook? Maybe. But there were other, more well-known public places with the necessary atmosphere and landmarks that would have served her purpose just as well — Golden Gate Park, Ocean Beach, the Marina Green, Coit Tower. Why Baker Beach? Why Lands End?

Suppose she hadn't picked them herself, but had had help from somebody who knew the city better than she did. Somebody to share the thrill of her little game. An accomplice if not a coconspirator. A lover.

The same somebody who'd picked Lake Merced as the place to dump her body and abandon her car: her murderer.

Vincent Canaday?

He'd lived in San Francisco. He'd been her lover for years. And he'd been incommunicado lately. . . .

I warned myself not to jump to conclusions. I could be way off base here, manufacturing suppositions to fit Canaday because I wanted him to be guilty. But the feeling persisted that Baker Beach and Lands End had been suggested or chosen by somebody other than Verity Daniels.

Which raised another question. If she'd had an accomplice, and she must have to make that fake recording for her lawyer, why hadn't she used him to pretend to be the extortionist caller in the first place? Let Runyon hear an actual recorded voice, make her hoax story even more plausible, instead of pretending to accidentally disconnect the recording interface? Even in the unlikely event the individual was a woman, you couldn't tell the gender of a caller if the right kind of filter was used.

Now something else had begun to nag at me, the kind of memory flicker that keeps eluding you the harder you try to recall it. Something I'd read or heard about Verity Daniels that might be significant if it were viewed in the right way. I read Runyon's report one more time, then Tamara's again. Nothing there triggered a recall. Something somebody had said, maybe?

Whatever it was, I couldn't get hold of it.

■ ■ ■ ■

I did not sleep well that night. Lay awake for a long time, while Kerry slept deeply beside me, unable to shut down the mental engines. And when I did finally drift off, I had the old nightmare again — a distorted, subconscious replay of the three months I'd spent shackled to the mountain cabin wall and left there to die.

Only this one was different. Relentless, episodic: I woke up twice, drenched in sweat, only to be dragged back into its depths. And I was not alone in the cabin. Kerry was there, wrapped and bound like a mummy, her terrified eyes staring up at me, pleading, but I couldn't reach her, help her because the chain was too short. Runyon was there, too, trapped in a cage no larger than a closet, his big hands clutching and shaking the bars while the cage slowly contracted around him. And the chain wouldn't let me reach him, either.

22

There was no way I was going to spend another day hanging and rattling in the city, going through motions, waiting for something to happen. The nightmare had left me tense, raw-nerved; I needed movement, aggressive purpose. Vincent Canaday still hadn't gone back to work at Gateway Insurance, still wasn't answering his cell or his home phone. But he was the best lead I had, and he had to be somewhere. Holed up in his house, avoiding people, was the most likely prospect. At least it was a place to start. And if I couldn't find Canaday, I'd have another shot at Hank Avery — keep him on the list of suspects or eliminate him, if I had to use threats or roughhouse methods to do it.

I let Tamara know by phone where I was going, rather than stopping at the agency on my way to the Bay Bridge. It was a few minutes past ten when I pulled up in front of Canaday's home in the Lafayette hills. Mine was the only car parked anywhere in the immediate vicinity, except for a gardener's truck and trailer farther up the block. The pulsing whine of a leaf blower made me clench my teeth as I went to the front gate, opened it, stepped into the front patio. There are a few unbearably loud, intrusive noises I hate more in this clamorous world than any others, and those created by leaf blowers top the list above backup beepers, chain saws, and electric hedge trimmers.

The patio was empty. So was the driveway in front of the matching stucco garage and its closed overhead doors. I went up the tile stairs and rang the bell four times. I couldn't hear the chimes inside this time because of the damn blower, but it didn't matter; they were either echoing in empty rooms or being ignored.

Down off the steps, across the patio to the driveway. So I was trespassing — the hell with it. The near-side wall of the garage was a smooth blank, no windows or doors. But there had to be another entrance besides the doors in front. I moved at an angle to the rear, where more yuccas and rows of bird-of-paradise plants partially screened a rear patio. When I rounded the corner there it was, a door recessed into the rear garage wall.

The door was closed, but when I pressed a decorative wrought-iron latch, it opened into oil-scented gloom. Plenty of room for two cars in there; now there was just one, drawn up in the middle of the concrete floor. Enough sunlight spilled in through the open doorway to let me see that the vehicle was a light-colored four-door sedan. I went in, around to the front, and squatted there. The light color was tan, the make was Chrysler, the model Town and Country. And the personalized license plate read GWAYINS.

Canaday was here, all right.

I backed out of the garage, shut the door. The leaf blower racket had stopped; it was quiet now except bird cries and distant street sounds. I made my way through the jungly profusion of plantings onto the rear patio. An inlaid tile fountain rose up in the middle of it, water trickling down into a squared off trough, which in turn trickled into a koi pond on one side. Fish swam murkily and sluggishly underneath a skim of green algae in the pond.

After half a dozen steps I could see the rear of the house under the overhang of a second-floor balcony. There were two sets of French doors, the larger of the sets closed and flanked by draped windows; the smaller, toward the far side, stood wide open. When I got over there, I could see into what looked to be an unlighted office: desk littered with stacks of loose papers, computer workstation, some furniture. A couple of steps closer and I could see the man sitting in the half light, not at the desk but on a leather couch set an angle opposite.

He wasn't doing anything, just sitting there with his hands knuckled together between his thighs. Unmoving, like a piece of statuary propped up for show. I climbed a single step to within a couple of paces of the open doorway. From there I had a better look at him. Forties, ruddy complexion, yellowish gray hair that hadn't been combed recently; wearing a short-sleeved sports shirt and a pair of rumpled slacks, his feet bare. His eyes were open and staring outward, but not at me. He didn't know I was there until I moved up next to one of the open door halves, rapped on it, and called out, "Mr. Canaday?"

Even then it was a couple of seconds before the knock and the sound of my voice registered. Then he blinked, shifted position slightly, but not as if he were startled to find that he had company.

"I thought you might be here," I said. "I rang the bell several times."

Six-beat. Then, in a voice without inflection or animation, like one generated by a computer, "Who're you? Police?"

"No. Were you expecting the police?"

No answer.

"It's important I talk to you. All right if I come in?"

"Go away, leave me alone."

I went in anyway. Even with the French doors open, the room had a dusty, boozy smell sharp enough to dilate my nostrils. There was an empty bottle of Scotch lying on its side next to the couch, a spill from it staining a portion of a mostly white Navaho rug. Another bottle, half full, and an empty glass stood on an end table. Now that I was inside out of the sunlight and shadow, I could see irregular patches of beard stubble on Canaday's face, discolored pouches under bleary eyes, another liquor stain on the front of his shirt. Two- or three-day bender, I thought. Though if he was drunk now, he wasn't far enough gone to slur his words.

"Go away," he said again.

"Not until we talk."

"No right to be here. Leave me alone."

I said, "Verity Daniels."

He reacted to the name, the first real sign of life he'd shown. His head jerked, his eyelids went up and down in little birdlike flutters; he leaned forward, squinting up, as if seeing me for the first time.

"Who are you?"

I told him. "Your relationship with her — that's why I'm here."

"She's dead," he said, and there was what sounded like genuine pain in the words. "Somebody killed her."

"The police think it was an associate of mine, but they're wrong. Jake Runyon is innocent."

"Runyon." Blankly. Then, "Her lover?"

"No. But you were, for years. Before and after her inheritance. Your idea, or was it the other way around? She pressure you into the affair?"

"Pressure?"

"Your insurance tricks."

". . . I don't know what you're talking about."

No, he didn't. His blank, muddled look made that plain enough. So she hadn't caught him defrauding one of his companies; just another of her fabrications. He'd been the aggressor in their relationship, not her.

"I loved her," he said after a little time.

"But she didn't love me anymore. All the things I did for her, and she wouldn't help me when I needed her the most."

"Help you how? Loan you money?"

"Rich, for God's sake, she could afford twenty thousand . . . I'd have paid back both loans. But she said no, ten thousand was all I'd ever get out of her."

"When was this?"

"Last week. Last Friday. Last chance."

"The ten thousand. When did she give you that?"

"Wasn't enough. I thought it would be, but it wasn't."

"When, Canaday?"

"Right after she inherited, moved to the city. No problem then . . . she still cared then. But then she changed."

"How did she change?"

"New life, new lover. New world that didn't include me."

"The new lover. Who?"

Headshake. "Always had to have a man. Bed partners, another husband when I couldn't marry her. All right for a while after Avery drowned . . . just me, I was enough for her until that money, all that goddamn money. . . ."

"Listen to me. Who was her new lover?"

"Wouldn't tell me his name. Somebody

close by, that's all she'd say. Always like that with her. Secrets. Lies. Games."

"Maybe she was lying. Making up the new lover as an excuse to break things off with you."

He didn't seem to hear me. "The screwing you get for the screwing you got," he said.

"Why did you kill her, Canaday?"

". . . What?"

"Because she wouldn't loan you the twenty thousand? Because she didn't want anything more to do with you?"

"You think I killed her?"

"Didn't you?"

"No. Me? No!"

He reached out blindly for the bottle of Scotch, almost knocked it over, caught it in time, and hauled it to him with both hands. Took a long pull, shuddering as he swallowed. Started to set the bottle back on the table, then changed his mind and cradled it against his chest with one hand. With the other he raked fingernails down along one unshaven cheek, hard enough to leave marks, as if trying to inflict pain on himself.

"I loved her," he said again. "Tore me up when I found out she was dead. Even after the way she treated me, all her lies, all her crap, I never stopped loving her. Wouldn't hurt her. Couldn't. Never."

The denial and the emotions behind it seemed genuine enough, but sober, calculating individuals like Verity Daniels aren't the only ones who can lie expertly. Maudlin drunks can manage it, too, if their guilt is too great and their desire for self-preservation strong enough.

I said, "If you loved her so much, why didn't you divorce your wife and marry her? Or didn't she want that?"

"She wanted it. Divorced her husband so we could."

She divorced Ostrander? No, but that must be the reason she'd told him about the affair — to force him to divorce her.

"But I couldn't do it," Canaday said. "I couldn't. My business, everything I worked for . . . Nancy would've gutted me financially, taken Susie away."

"Your wife and daughter are gone now, aren't they?"

Muscles rippled along his jaw, creating a facial tic that lasted for several seconds. His eyes had that vacant stare again.

"Because she found out about you and Verity Daniels? Is that why she left you?"

Headshake. "All those years . . . Nancy never knew about us. Or any of the others until that stupid one-night stand . . . but

Christ, when it falls into your lap, you take it, don't you? Don't you?"

I didn't say anything.

Canaday was silent, too, for several beats. Then, in a low mutter, "But Nancy didn't really care. Excuse, that's all. Money, money, always money. Hated the idea of being poor again. Ready to leave for a long time. Rat deserting a sinking ship."

Oozing self-pity. Making excuses for his behavior, his shortcomings, while condemning those made by his wife and his mistress.

I said, "If you didn't strangle Verity Daniels, who did? The new lover, if she had one?"

Headshake. A little bulb of spittle appeared at one corner of his mouth, broke and trickled down over his chin.

"My money's still on you, Canaday."

No reaction at all this time, except to take another long swallow from the bottle. It must have burned going down because he coughed, grimaced, then thrust the bottle away to the table. It tipped over when he let go, rolled off onto the rug.

"You'll talk to the police," I said. "If you did kill her, they'll get it out of you. One way or another."

He'd stopped listening again. Abruptly he shoved onto his feet, made his way in a

281

groping stagger past me to the cluttered desk. Sat down hard in the chair and began pawing among the litter of papers.

"Gone," he said, "all gone."

"What's all gone?"

"Too late, all gone." More drool crawled out of his mouth. "Knew it two days ago, couldn't make myself do it, but now . . . now . . ."

"Do what?"

I should not have had to ask that question; I should have realized what he was doing. But I didn't until I saw the gun come out, and then it was too late.

All in one motion, with no hesitation, he dragged it from under the pile of papers, brought the long barrel up under his chin, and pulled the trigger.

I've seen men die before, more than once, but not like this. Not while I stood flat-footed, a cry stillborn in my throat, helplessly watching Canaday's head explode like a fireworks fountain, blood and gore geysering and spraying, the gun clattering against the desk, his body toppling sideways in the chair. The after-echo of the shot reverberated off the walls, the stink of cordite and loosened bowels fouled the air.

Bile spewed into the back of my throat; I had to lock the muscles to keep it down, and at that I almost didn't get out of that room in time, in a twisting lunge through the open French doors into the fresh hot late-summer breeze. I stood there on the patio tiles, bent over a little, until I was sure I wouldn't throw up. Then I began taking deep breaths to clear my lungs, my nostrils, my head. Telling myself I couldn't have known about the gun, couldn't have foreseen that Canaday had been nerving himself up to suicide, couldn't have stopped him in those last few seconds even if I'd caught on to what he intended to do.

None of it made me feel any less sick.

23

You do what you have to in situations like this. Whatever you have to do.

Before anything else, I called 911 and reported the suicide. Name and address of the deceased, my name and profession — that was all the information I gave to the operator. Yes, I would wait for officers to arrive. No, I hadn't touched nor would I touch anything.

That last was a small lie. I stood on the patio for maybe a minute after disconnecting, to determine if any of the neighbors had heard the shot and would come to investigate. None had, evidently; no heads appeared above the hedges bordering the yard, the front door chimes didn't go off, the neighborhood was as drowsily quiet as it had been before Canaday blew himself away. In the midst of death, life goes on unawares. Then I steeled myself and went back inside the office.

The stench in there may still have been as strong, but I was mouth-breathing now so I wouldn't have to smell it. I went around the side of the desk. One look at Canaday and the splatters on the whitewashed stucco wall behind him was all I allowed myself. The slug's impact and the jerking weight of his body had kicked the chair backward a couple of feet; he was half sitting, half lying sideways across one armrest, what was left of his head tilted at a grotesque angle. The gun had jarred loose when his arm flopped down against the desk's edge, lay at his feet. An old .41 Magnum, from the look of it. No wonder the bullet had torn his skull apart.

There was no gore on the floor between him and the desk; he'd fired at just enough of a backward angle so that all except for random droplets was behind him. I wedged myself into the space, my back to the body, and bent to look at the scatter of papers on the top.

Financial records, mostly, at least those in plain sight. I fished a pencil out of a leather-wrapped canister, inverted it and used the eraser to move the papers around. One of those underneath was a vellum sheet with Canaday's personal letterhead imprinted at the top. Shaky, down-slanted handwriting filled the upper third.

Nancy —
You made me do this. You and your demands, your coldness in bed, your love of money, if you'd stuck by me I could have found a way to go on but now it's too late I can't

That was all. Unfinished suicide note, blame-shifting, pathetic. And no mention of Verity Daniels.

There was nothing else of a personal nature among the papers. Using my handkerchief, I opened the desk drawers one by one. Nothing in any of them that connected Canaday with Daniels in any way.

Still quiet outside, except for birdsong and the distant barking of a dog. But the minions would be here pretty soon now. I took a turn around the office, avoiding eye contact with Canaday's remains and the wall behind him. Not expecting to find anything; not finding anything. I thought about looking through the rest of the house, but there wouldn't be enough time for a thorough search, and even if there had been it would probably be an exercise in futility. Anything to do with the dead woman would've been in here, his private space.

Had Canaday killed Daniels? No reason for him to lie about it with suicide on his mind . . . unless he'd been unable to put words to the guilt that was eating at him. Plenty of other reasons for him to take the coward's way out: financial ruin, abandonment by his wife, loss of his child, loss of the mistress he'd loved. Murder didn't have to be one of them.

Let it be Canaday, I thought. Let it end right here.

But my gut feeling was that it wouldn't.

The Lafayette police kept me around for a little under two hours before they let me go. Except for a couple of rounds of Q&A, the first with a pair of uniforms in the patrol unit that responded to the call, the second with a plainclothes investigator, I sat under the oak tree in the front patio and waited. All the officers were efficient, polite, respectful. I felt bad about lying to them, even though the lies were minor enough. Sins of omission, really.

I did not own up to being in the room with Canaday when he shot himself; I said that my conversation with him had lasted only three or four minutes, and that I'd just left through the open French doors and was coming around to the front of the house when I heard the gun go off inside. Then I'd run back to the office, found Canaday dead, and immediately called 911. About everything else, my reasons for being there, the investigation I was pursuing, my failure to interpret the man's drunkenness as a prelude to suicide, I was completely truthful. The sins of omission were necessary, I felt, to avoid detailed explanations and any suspicions the law might have had that I was the cause, direct or indirect, of Canaday's self-destruction. They didn't need to know that I'd witnessed it, or exactly what information I'd gotten from him beforehand. But the main reason was, I had no desire to verbally relive any of that time in the company of a man alive one minute, dead the next.

They seemed to believe me; there was no reason why they shouldn't. Still, I worried a little while I sat there under the oak, waiting and chafing at the delay. Worried, and thought about different things to keep my mind focused and the memory screen blank.

Suicide was one of the things I thought about. I understand and empathize with an intolerably suffering cancer patient choosing to take his or her own life; I might do the same thing myself if I were ever in that unbearable condition, despite my Catholic upbringing. But the other kind of self-destruction, Canaday's kind, I do not understand or condone. It's the ultimate selfish, craven act of a person so wrapped up in his own misery that he neither thinks of nor cares about those whose lives are affected by his cowardice. In Canaday's case, his daughter, if not his wife. Other relatives. Friends. The women who worked for him at Gateway Insurance. The companies he represented, his individual clients. There's always somebody left behind who gets hurt in one way or another. And always somebody who has to come in to clean up the mess.

Over the years I've had dealings with all sorts of individuals struggling to survive. None of them had given up and taken the easy way out; no matter how hard things got, they hung on with both hands to life, love, faith, hope. Same with the millions more in this and other countries, those whose struggles I was aware of and those I would never hear about.

No one goes through their time on this earth error-free, sin-free, unsullied and unscathed, not even the powerbrokers or the uber-rich or the holier-than-thou religious right. We all suffer to one degree or another. As far as I'm concerned, the scattered few like Vincent Canaday who quit in mid-conflict, who throw away their most precious gift at the expense of others, deserve neither pity nor sorrow, but only contempt.

Before I drove back to the city, I called Tamara to tell her what had happened and what I'd found out from Canaday. But not that I'd been in the room with him when he blew his head apart. She had no need to know the literal truth any more than the Lafayette cops or anybody else did. What I'd seen in that office was a thing to be shared with no one, now or ever — another link in the chain of large and small horrors that belonged only to me.

"See if you can get hold of Dragovich," I said, "and fill him in. I'll stop at the Hall and do the same with Figone and Samuels. If Canaday murdered Verity Daniels, they're the ones to dig it out with the cooperation of the Lafayette cops."

"Yeah, if they follow up."

"They will. They're pros and they don't want Jake to be guilty any more than we do."

"*Did* Canaday do it?"

"Make it easier on all of us if he did."

"But you don't think so?"

"Leaning against it. The way he talked about Daniels, how much he loved her, how he'd never have hurt her . . . He could've been lying, but why? He was ready to die, I wish to Christ I'd realized how ready — he had no reason not to come clean if he was shouldering that kind of guilt."

"Unless that's the real reason he offed himself."

"Her death, yes, that was part of it. But he talked freely enough about his wife leaving him, his financial troubles, his relationship with Daniels. I just didn't get the impression he was holding anything back."

"So if he didn't do it, all we've got is this new lover of hers."

"If he exists."

"It'd explain where she went all those early mornings and on weekends the past couple of months."

"Yes, it would. Clandestine meetings somewhere."

"Why wouldn't they just get it on in her condo?"

"Hard to tell with her. Married man, maybe, and he was afraid of being seen with her."

"Somebody close by — that's what she told Canaday, right?"

"All she'd tell him, he said."

291

"Must be another resident of Bayfront Towers. Up until two months ago Daniels never did much of anything except sit in her condo and watch TV, and think up stupid games to play."

"Not necessarily. She went out to eat, buy necessities. She could've met someone in the neighborhood. Bayfront isn't the only condo building in that area."

"Well, we better hope it's somebody in Bayfront. Otherwise, how do we find him?"

I had nothing to say to that.

"What about the guy who hit on her in the elevator, Weatherford?" Tamara said. "Maybe she didn't say no after all, and he lied to save his ass."

"Worth checking on. He's the CEO at what company?"

"TechPerfect, on New Montgomery."

"Call them up and find out if he'll see me. Either there or at his condo, asap."

"Probably have to go through a gate-keeper. Should I say why you want to talk to him?"

"Just that it pertains to the murder of Verity Daniels."

"What if he refuses?"

"Then we'll know something right there, won't we?"

■ ■ ■ ■

I came off the Bay Bridge in the shadow of the Hall of Justice and made that my first stop. Samuels and Figone were both away from their desks in the homicide division, but expected back shortly. I went from there to the main jail. Visiting hours were still in effect, so they let me see Runyon without any hassle.

Locked down twice, I thought when they brought him out. Inside his cell and inside himself. His way of coping with any difficult situation, and one I sometimes wished I could emulate. But I didn't have the discipline or the patience for it. If I'd been in his shoes, I would have been climbing the walls by this time.

His neutral expression didn't change when I laid out the latest developments. "But you don't think Canaday killed Daniels," he said. It wasn't a question.

"Hoping it turns out that way, but . . . no, I don't. Or that Hank Avery's our man. No solid motive and no ties to the city. It figures to be somebody who knows the city well." I told him my suppositions about Lake Merced and Daniels having had help in picking Baker Beach and Lands End.

"Makes sense."

"Canaday might qualify from the short time he lived here, but a native or long-time resident is more likely."

"The new lover."

"Have to bank on that possibility for now. You're sure Daniels never mentioned Chad Weatherford's name? He's a native San Franciscan. Or anybody else's name, even in passing?"

"Positive. I'd remember if she had."

"What about places in the neighborhood where she might have met somebody?"

Runyon thought about it. "A couple of well-known restaurants, that's all. No bars or clubs."

I asked him which restaurants and made a mental note of the names. Popular places, always crowded for lunch and dinner. Not much chance any staff members or regular customers would remember Verity Daniels and a man she'd met or dined with, but if I ran out of other leads I'd make the rounds of those places and others in the neighborhood.

Jim Figone was at his desk when I left Runyon and went back to the homicide division. I replayed Canaday's suicide and connection to Verity Daniels for him, not offering any opinions, just laying out the facts.

He listened with interest, said he'd follow up with the Lafayette PD and let me know if any evidence came to light that linked Canaday to Daniels's murder. He didn't say he hoped it would turn out that way, but I had the impression he was thinking it. I also had the impression that he shared my gloomy doubts that it would.

At the agency Tamara said, "Got you an appointment with Weatherford. Tomorrow morning, eleven-fifty, his office at TechPerfect." Her mouth quirked sardonically. "And make sure you're on time — man can't spare you more than ten minutes."

"You speak to him personally?"

"For about thirty seconds. I hard-lined his gatekeeper until she put me through."

"He seem cooperative?"

"Wouldn't know it from the way he talked. Snotty cool. Tell you one thing I didn't need more than the thirty seconds to figure out."

"What's that?"

"The man's an asshole."

I had trouble sleeping again that night. Too tensed up. I would have liked to make love to Kerry, for the closeness as much as the stress release, but she didn't seem to want to be held and I was not about to try to convince her. She was still fragile, still healing. Until she was whole again, the initiative would have to remain hers.

So I lay there wired in the dark, holding her hand, thoughts running around inside my head, knowing without thinking about it that the reason I couldn't sleep was that I was afraid to, because I knew what my subconscious would have waiting for me.

And that was just what happened when I finally dropped off — Vincent Canaday's head exploding again on the flickering screen of nightmare.

24

I've learned to take Tamara's impulsive judgments with a grain of salt, but her assessment of Chad Weatherford's character proved to be right on. He was an asshole, all right. One of these young corporate executives so devoted to the enrichment of self and self-image that they develop what you might call a minor deity complex. They view everyone who comes within their sphere as inferiors and pawns to be used for professional gain and personal gratification. They care little or nothing about anyone who is of no benefit to them; fail to do their bidding or cross them in any way and they'll heap wrath on you and sweep you aside without a second thought. If TechPerfect ever grew into a corporate giant and Weatherford remained at the helm, the minor deity thing would no doubt evolve into a full-fledged God complex.

When and if the Weatherfords of the world

grant small favors to strangers, it's either for their advantage or because it puffs up their ego by making them feel magnanimous. The latter was the only reason, if in fact he was innocent of any complicity in Verity Daniels's murder, that he'd agreed to talk to me. He didn't give a damn that a woman and neighbor was dead by violence or that an innocent man's liberty and reputation were in jeopardy. He had more vital things on his mind. Yes, he did. The perpetuation and prosperity of Chad Weatherford and his aggressive little kingdom was uppermost, but there were others, too, almost as important in his view.

Such as his daily exercise regimen.

He made that clear to me as soon as I was shown into his walnut-paneled, apartment-sized office at TechPerfect's corporate headquarters. Among a lot of expensive furnishings was one of those stair-climbing exercise machines, and he was hooked up to it and energetically striding away on it. Dressed in sweats and tennis shoes, a towel draped around his neck, sweat beading his lean, sharp-jawed face. He saw no reason to stop or even slow down for the likes of me, no reason to offer a cordial greeting, to shake my hand, to invite me to have a seat. Just kept right on pumping away while he enlightened me.

"Give you ten minutes max," he said without preamble. "Tight schedule this morning, just managed to squeeze you in. Too busy to get enough exercise these days, have to grab a few minutes here whenever I can. Keep in shape."

He was already in shape, as far as I could tell. The sweats he wore were tight-fitting and showed off the muscles working in his legs and shoulders. Not exactly a pretty boy, but with the kind of dark-haired, dark-complexioned, virile good looks that had a magnetic attraction for women. He'd never want for female worshippers and acolytes to fill his bed and feed his self-esteem.

I said, civilly enough, "You know why I'm here, Mr. Weatherford."

"Naturally. Daniels woman. Don't see how I can help you. Already told the police all I know about her."

"Tell me, if you don't mind."

He didn't answer immediately because he was checking dials on the machine — pedometer, pulse rate, whatever. Smiling to himself while he did it: the minor deity was having a good day.

"Nothing to tell, really. Met her in the elevator at my building." His building, as if he owned all of Bayfront Towers. "Nice looking. Nice body. Talked her up, invited her to dinner. No dice. You know how it is — win some, lose some."

"And that's the only contact you had with her."

"No reason to have any more. Saw her a couple of times after that, didn't talk to her."

"Where did you see her?"

"Building. Garage, lobby."

"Nowhere else?"

"No."

"Was she with anybody any of those times?"

"No."

"So as far as you know, she wasn't dating anyone who lives in Bayfront Towers."

"Far as I know. None of my business."

"How did she act that day in the elevator?"

"Evening, not day. Just after I got home."

"All right, then, evening."

Weatherford made another check of the stair-stepper dials, increased his speed on the pedals to a kind of spurting run. "Almost done. Couple more minutes, then just enough time to grab a quick shower before lunch."

He'd begun to rub on me like sandpaper on a raw nerve. "You haven't answered my question, Mr. Weatherford."

"What question is that?"

"How Verity Daniels acted in the elevator."

"What do you mean, acted?"

"Her demeanor. Aloof, friendly, flirtatious?"

"None of the above. Frosty. Not really my type anyway."

His type, I thought, would be the instantly adoring and easily seduced. I said, "Exactly what did you talk about?"

"Who remembers? I looked her over, she had a nice body like I said, I suggested dinner, she said no thanks. End of story."

"Did she give you the impression she wasn't available to anyone or just not to you?"

He didn't like that; it put a hitch in his energetic workout. "What kind of question is that?"

"A reasonable one. Don't take it personally. Did she seem available?"

"Wouldn't have asked her out if I didn't think so. No sense wasting my time otherwise. Maybe she was a bottom feeder. Who knows?"

"Why would you say that?"

"Say what?"

"Bottom feeder. Meaning what?"

"Nouveau riche, wasn't she? Secretary or

something before she inherited money?"

"Oh, I get it. You think she might have turned you down because she was uncomfortable with men of your class."

The subtle sarcasm was wasted on Weatherford. He said, "Right. Uncomfortable, overwhelmed. Preferred men who wear uniforms and carry clipboards."

"Uniforms and clipboards?"

He glanced at his watch again, nodded his head vigorously, and quit exercising. Blew out his breath and then began toweling the sweat off his face. "Time's up," he said.

"Not just yet," I said. "Not until you tell me what you meant by a preference for uniforms and clipboards."

"Maybe you didn't hear me. I said time's up."

"Maybe you didn't hear *me*. Uniforms and clipboards."

He was looking at me now, really looking at me for the first time. "I don't care for your attitude."

I managed to avoid making the obvious response. "Uniforms and clipboards, Mr. Weatherford."

"Oh, for Christ's sake. She was all over Frank one day when I drove in."

"Frank?"

"Garage security man, evening shift. Rub-

302

bing her tits on his arm, laughing about something."

Frank Krikowski. "You told me before you hadn't seen Verity Daniels with anyone at Bayfront Towers."

"Not with any resident," Weatherford said. "Frank just works there. He's just a security guard."

Security guard.

Verity Daniels and Frank Krikowski.

Sure, it made sense. Somebody close by . . . somebody at Bayfront Towers, but not one of the residents. She'd been a small-salaried employee most of her life, and except for Vincent Canaday, her past associations had been with working-class men: Scott Ostrander, Jason Avery. Canaday was the only professional man she'd been involved with, and the nature of her on-again, off-again affair with him might well have soured her on his type. An illicit affair with a macho security guard in her own building would have been right up her alley.

She talks a good fight, keeps saying over and over in a giggly little voice that she's on her guard. Runyon's comment during our three-way conference call with Tamara — that was the memory fragment I'd been trying to recall, and that might have tipped me sooner if I had. Why would Daniels have kept saying over and over that she was on her guard, when she had no real reason to be? And why would she giggle when she was saying it? Answer: the phrase had another, literal meaning, a sly taunting of Runyon with a sexual reference to her new lover and accomplice. "On her guard" had meant just that, being on top of her security guard in bed.

Krikowski lived in San Francisco and had for the past fifteen years. Tamara pulled up his address — 27th Street on the southern edge of the Mission, near S.F. General — and some background data on him in less than ten minutes. Clean record: he'd worked in law enforcement down the Peninsula for four years, spent the last nine as a private security guard for the corporation that owned Bayfront Towers and several similar buildings; had been employed at Bayfront since it opened. Married ten years, two children. Debts like most of us these days, but not swimming in them; mostly he managed to pay his bills on time.

No red flags in any of that, but I'd had more than enough experience not to put too much stock in surfaces. Some people used marriage and respectability to camouflage all sorts of illegal and immoral activities — people like Vincent Canaday. Others were exactly what they seemed to be until something — or someone like Verity Daniels — pushed them over onto the dark side.

The woman who opened the door of the flat on 27th Street was a tired-looking brunette wearing sweatshirt, jeans, and long dangly earrings that didn't go with her outfit or her plump features. Frank Krikowski's wife. Yes, her husband was home, he didn't leave for work until three-thirty. What did I want to see him about? I started to tell her it was a private matter when an infant began a loud squalling somewhere inside.

"My God," she said, "there he goes again. That kid never lets me have a minute's peace." She backed up into the room behind her, shouted, "Frank! Somebody to see you," and vanished leaving the door open.

I heard him say, "Who is it?" and her answer, "I don't know, I never saw him before," and a couple of seconds later Krikowski appeared. He wore his uniform pants, an unbuttoned shirt hanging loose above them.

One look at me and his mouth pinched in at the corners; he had a good memory for faces. "You never give up, do you? Now what do you want?"

"Few minutes of your time."

"You already had that at Bayfront. I can't tell you any more now than I could then."

"Step outside, Mr. Krikowski, so we can talk in private."

"Listen, I don't appreciate being bothered at home like this." Inside, his wife's ministrations to the infant were having no effect; the squalling had escalated into a series of wailing shrieks. "I can't hear myself think when Frankie goes off like that. I always wanted a son, what I got was a screamer."

I didn't say anything.

He looked at me, winced as the shrieking climbed another couple of decibels. "Christ! All right," he said, and came out onto the narrow porch and shut the door behind him. "Well?"

"Verity Daniels. How well did you know her?"

"What do you mean, how well? She was a resident, I said hello to her when she drove in or out, that's all."

"That's not what I've been told."

He was frowning now, but in a bemused way. "Told what?"

"That you had something going with her."

"That I . . . Jesus! Ms. Daniels and me? Who told you that?"

"Another resident saw you together in the

garage one afternoon. Said you were all over each other."

"That's a damn lie!"

"She was holding on to your arm, rubbing herself against you. Sounds pretty intimate to me."

"Who the hell . . . oh, yeah, now I get it. Mr. Weatherford. Big shot, smart guy. He's the one, isn't he?"

"You deny it happened?"

"No, it happened, but it wasn't my fault. Weatherford drove in, he saw it, he made a smart remark to me the next day about how she was a nice piece but I ought to be more careful about groping the residents in public. I told him it was her did the groping, but he just laughed, said don't worry, he wouldn't report me."

"You're saying Verity Daniels came on to you?"

"That's right. Made it real plain we could have some fun, and gave me a little sample that time. I'm no Brad Pitt but she wasn't the first. Some of these rich women, and not just the single ones, they're always on the make. I won't say I never been tempted, but I don't screw around on my wife, and even if I did, I'd have to be six kinds of nuts to do it where I work."

"So you turned her down."

"Flat, same as the others before her. Polite as I know how, so she wouldn't try to get me in trouble. Said I was flattered, she was a nice lady — a lie, she always seemed a little weird to me — but I loved my wife and believed in my marriage vows."

"And what did she say?"

"Got a little hot at first, called me a couple of names. I just stood there and took it. Then she calmed down and said she bet George wouldn't say no, like she was trying to make me jealous. I didn't bite on that, either. And that was the end of it. She pretty much ignored me after that, God's honest truth."

"George," I said. "George Haxner?"

"Yeah."

"Friendly with him, too?"

"Pretty friendly. But if she put the moves on him, he never said anything to me about it."

"Closed-mouth type?"

"Well, he never used to be. Bragged to me once about a woman he'd had on one of his other security jobs."

"He say anything at all to you about Verity Daniels?"

"That she was a real fox, right after she moved in."

"But nothing after you turned her down."

"Not until we heard she'd been murdered. Everybody was talking about her then."

"Did you tell him about Verity Daniels coming on to you?"

"No way. Nobody's business but mine and hers." Krikowski let out a heavy sighing breath. "That's what I figured until now, anyhow."

"What about the police? You tell them?"

"And have them start looking my way, like you're doing? No, sir. They had enough evidence to arrest Jake Runyon so I figured he must be guilty. If you think I had anything to do it with it, you're crazy."

No, I didn't think he did. Not anymore. But I asked, "Can you account for your whereabouts Saturday from four-thirty on?"

"You bet I can. My mother came in to take care of the kids and Fran and me went to her brother's in San Mateo for dinner. Stayed until about eleven, came home, talked awhile, went to bed. That satisfy you?"

"Yes."

"So now you go bugging George, I suppose. Grabbing at straws, man, if you ask me."

That could be. But I was thinking: Daniels and her sensation-fueled games. In her skewed world, everything had been about manipulation, control, excitement. If she couldn't score with one security guard, another would do just as well. A big mistake that had cost her her life.

25

The information Tamara pulled up on George Haxner was just what I wanted to hear. Born and raised in South San Francisco. Patrol cop in S.F. for four years, dismissed for use of excessive force on a teenage robbery suspect. Security work ever since, and his record none too spotless there, either: fired from one job with a large manufacturing company in the South Bay for making improper advances to a woman employee. Arrested once five years ago for a domestic disturbance involving his ex-wife, assault charges dropped when the victim changed her mind and withdrew the complaint. Divorced shortly thereafter. Lived alone since, in the same rented house he'd shared with the ex.

And the clincher: the house was located on Shields Street on San Francisco's west side, not much more than a couple of miles from Lake Merced Boulevard — walking distance from the parking area where Verity Daniels's BMW had been abandoned.

Haxner, all right.

Now I had to find a way to prove it.

The neighborhood where George Haxner lived was old San Francisco working class, not unlike the one I'd grown up in in the Outer Mission a few miles away. It had changed some over the years, become desirable to less affluent urbanites because the home prices were reasonable in comparison to those in other parts of the city and because of its proximity to Lake Merced and the ocean, the S.F. State campus, the Stonestown shopping mall.

Haxner's rented house was the kind that real-estate agents describe as a "fixer-upper" — a small clapboard structure, not much larger than a cottage, with walls and trim that would have needed three coats of paint to make presentable and a front yard full of gravel and dead grass. Its cracked asphalt driveway was empty when I pulled up in front a little before three. Yellowed Venetian blinds covered the front windows. On the narrow little porch, dessicated plant corpses occupied a pair of cracked terra cotta urns flanking the door. Home sweet home.

I rang the bell three times without getting an answer. Haxner must have left for work early, or had some kind of errand to run on the way. Bayfront Towers was on the other side of the city, but unless he ran into heavy traffic, it wouldn't take him more than forty minutes to get there from here.

I felt edgy, disgruntled, as I returned to the car. Thinking that I should have remembered the "on my guard" business sooner, made the connection sooner. Thinking I'd been too focused on the men in Verity Daniels's former life. Maybe. But the extortion flimflam and phony rape complaint and nuisance lawsuits had muddied the waters, and there'd been nothing else to point to a security guard, no good reason to even consider running routine background checks on any of them. Kicking myself for not being an omniscient master sleuth was pointless. Hell, it was a wonder Daniels's out-of-character taunt had lodged in my subconscious at all.

All right, what now? I did not want to have to brace Haxner at Bayfront Towers. Too public. I would have to walk a finer line with him than I had with Krikowski — phrase my questions carefully, try to get him to admit something incriminating without making any direct accusations. And even with that approach, there was no guarantee I could get enough out of him to convince Figone and Samuels that I was on the right track.

A neighborhood canvass was a better idea. The logical place for Haxner and Verity Daniels to have done their trysting was in this rundown rental house of his. It had the required privacy, plus it explained where Daniels had disappeared to for several hours two and three mornings a week and on weekends. If that was the case, then it was possible one of the neighbors had seen her arriving or leaving, or that distinctive BMW of hers parked in the vicinity.

No such luck. I rang nine doorbells and talked to five people, three of the five willing to answer my questions. All of them knew George Haxner by sight, but nothing much about him because he kept to himself and because, as one of them told me, folks on this street minded their own business. A woman in the house directly opposite said the only car she'd ever seen parked in Haxner's driveway was the green four-door sedan that belonged to him.

Almost five by the time I was done with the canvass, and the edgy frustration was sharper now. And breached by a worm of doubt. I'd been wrong about Krikowski being Daniels's lover; suppose I was wrong about Haxner, too? I didn't want to believe it. It *had* to be Haxner. Maybe they hadn't carried on their affair here after all. Or else they'd taken considerable pains to keep it a secret even from Haxner's neighbors, in which case the idea had to have been Daniels's. It was just the sort of melodramatic intrigue she'd gone in for.

Two options now. Go see Haxner at Bayfront Towers after all, or call it a day and come back here tomorrow morning. The problem with both was that I would be bracing him on his turf: the place he worked and the place he lived. He didn't have to talk to me at all if he didn't want to, especially not here at his house —

His house.

And inside it . . . what? Something that might link him to Daniels, maybe to her murder?

Sure, maybe. But in order to find out I would probably have to break-and-enter, and I was not willing to do that. Even if I were, it was still daylight and it took time to pick door and window locks, if they could be picked at all, and smashing a window was noisy as well as destructive.

Suppose he'd left one of the doors or windows unlocked?

Fat chance. Ex-cops were seldom that careless. And it would still be illegal trespass, not that I was above that kind of gamble; I'd done it before.

There was one other unlikely possibility. Check it out?

No. Forget it. Waste of time.

But even as I thought that, impulse drove me out of the car. None of the immediate neighbors was in sight and the street was empty. Better make this quick just the same. On the porch I tried the door first, with the expected result. The terra cotta urns were easy enough to tilt so that I could take quick looks underneath. Nothing but dirt. I rummaged among the dead plants inside one urn, didn't find anything, and moved over to the other. Nothing there, either —

Wait. Yes, there was.

Key. Pushed round end down into the dry soil among the stalks.

I pulled it out, stood there with it in my hand. New, still shiny under the flecks of dirt. Not a spare key, I thought — one he'd had made for Verity Daniels. I almost wished I hadn't found it. Almost. But now that I'd gotten lucky . . .

A car went by on the street, but the driver paid no attention to me as it rolled on out of sight. Still nobody on the sidewalks or in the nearby yards. And Haxner was at work on the other side of the city.

I slid the key into the lock, turned it, heard the bolt click over. And before I could change my mind I opened the door, walked in as if I belonged there, and then shut it behind me.

For a few seconds I stayed put to let my eyes adjust to the gloom. Living room. Air a little musty, as if the place hadn't had a good airing in some time. I got out the pencil flashlight I carry, shined it around. Old, nondescript furniture, older model TV set, a shabby carpet worn through in places. None of the usual bachelor's clutter; whatever else Haxner was, he cleaned up after himself. I opened drawers in the end tables flanking the sofa. A farrago of stuff, none of it of any interest. A cabinet stood against one wall, but all it contained was sets of dishes, glassware, and linens that looked as if they hadn't been used in years.

I moved on through a small dining room, then into the kitchen. Nothing in either one. A door opened into a utility room just large enough for a washer and dryer, and another door in there led into the attached garage. I didn't find anything in the utility room, but in the garage —

A folded length of plastic sheeting and a

coil of nylon rope, stuffed under a workbench along one wall. I dragged them out for a close look. The top edge of the plastic showed ragged where a piece had been snipped off, probably with the pair of shears that lay atop the bench. One end of the rope also showed a fresh diagonal cut.

Solid evidence, if both cuts matched those on the section of sheet and piece of rope that had been used to bind up Verity Daniels's corpse. But would it be enough to offset that damn coat button? Given the way defense attorneys worked and judges interpreted the fine points of the law these days, probably not.

I put the sheeting and rope back where I'd found them. There was nothing else for me in the garage; I went back into the house, down the hallway on the far side that led to a pair of bedrooms with a bathroom sandwiched between.

The nearest was no longer a bedroom; Haxner had turned it into a combination storage and exercise room. Mostly storage: a stack of cardboard boxes, a folded futon, a chair with a jagged tear in its upholstered backrest, an old wardrobe with nothing inside it but a couple of spiderwebs. A collection of barbells and weights had a dusty, disused look — the kind of equipment you see for sale cheap at yard and garage sales.

Five minutes poking around in there was enough. The adjacent bathroom was still a little moist from Haxner's prework shower, the air thick with the mingled smells of soap and lime-scented aftershave lotion. Usual stuff in the medicine cabinet, none of it feminine. The old patterned robe hanging from a hook behind the door was a man's. To be thorough, I lifted the lid on the toilet tank for a look inside. Common hiding place, but not one used by Haxner.

The bedroom at the rear had a big double bed with a mahogany headboard done in a bas-relief pattern of squares. The bed was unmade, but the blankets had been drawn halfway up. No bachelor's clutter here, either; enough light filtered in through a shaded rear window to let me see that. The top of a heavy oak bureau was empty except for a hairbrush and a small leather case. A digital alarm clock was the only item on the single nightstand. The few articles of clothing inside the closet were all on hangers and all male.

But there was something wrong with the way the room looked. I couldn't tell what it was until I risked switching on the overhead light. Then I had it. The carpet in there was wall-to-wall, a faded green with a nondescript pattern, and bare except for a oval, braided throw rug a couple of feet from the bed. The rug was what was wrong — it didn't belong there, so far away from the bed.

Another thing, too: there was no lamp on the nightstand.

I lifted one end of the rug, dragged it aside. A couple of Rorschach-like blots stained the carpet underneath. Haxner had tried to remove them with some kind of solvent, but it had done nothing more than blur and smear them. Professional carpet cleaners would have had a difficult time getting spilled blood out of an old carpet like this.

Verity Daniels's blood. This was where she'd been struck with the blunt instrument — a bedside lamp, for instance — and then strangled.

Conclusive proof, if a sample from the carpet matched her DNA.

I replaced the rug as I'd found it, then got down on hands and knees and looked under the bed. Dust bunnies. But when I used the backs of my hands to move the nightstand, light winked off a fragment of opaque glass wedged up against the baseboard. I leaned close to peer at it. Piece of broken light bulb. Something he'd missed when he cleaned up afterward.

I left the fragment where it was, maneuvered the nightstand back in place. Anything else in here?

The case on the bureau first. I opened it, using my handkerchief to avoid leaving fingerprints for the police to find. A couple of outmoded tie clips, a pair of cufflinks, a man's wedding ring, a handful of loose change. The bureau drawers held underwear, socks, T-shirts, two dress shirts in unopened cleaner bags. I pulled each one all the way out so I could look underneath. Nothing. A pad of paper, two pencils, a roll of breath mints, and a six-pack of Trojan condoms with two left unused occupied the nightstand drawer. Its underside hadn't been used as a hiding place, either.

I lifted the blankets and sheets on the bed and ran my hand between the mattress and the box springs. Nothing. I went around on the other side and did the same thing there. Nothing. Then I noticed that the headboard on that side was pushed up tight against the wall, while on the other side it stood out a couple of inches. Simple shifting from Haxner's weight, probably, though the headboard and frame looked heavy.

What I was seeing then was that pattern of squares, the two largest in the middle about six-by-eight inches each. Convex on this side . . . and on the other?

I tugged the one end away from the wall. The headboard wasn't as heavy as it looked — made of paneling fitted between the supports rather than solid wood. Didn't take much effort to wiggle it out far enough so that I could squeeze in behind. The squares were not solid pieces that had been attached to the outer portion; rather, they were molded, hollow sections of the paneling itself.

And inside one of the six-by-eight squares . . . a small cloth bag fastened to the wood with duct tape.

I peeled the bag loose, fingered its bulky contents through the cloth, then brought it out to where the light was better. It was the kind with a knotted drawstring to hold it closed. I loosened the knots, upended the bag into the palm of my other hand.

Thin platinum gold wristwatch with a gold-link band, the case engraved with *Verity* in flowing script. Blood-ruby gold ring. And a pair of dangly gold earrings.

Verity Daniels's missing jewelry.

Got you for sure now, Haxner. Dead-bang.

I slid the items back into the bag, closed and reknotted the drawstring, retaped the bag inside the hollow square exactly as I'd found it, and shoved the headboard back tight against the wall again. Everything I'd turned up had to be left where it was for the police to find with a search warrant. That meant I would have to do some fast talking to convince Figone and Samuels that Haxner was the perp, and do it without revealing specific information or the fact that I'd committed a felony to get it. It could be done if I handled it right. And for Runyon's sake, I damn well would.

That was what I was thinking as I switched off the light, quit the bedroom, hurried down the hallway. But when I came into the living room, the thought went right out of my head. I stopped as abruptly as if I'd walked into a wall.

George Haxner was standing flat-footed just inside the front door.

And the gun in his hand was aimed straight at my gullet.

26

You never get used to being on the wrong
end of a fire-arm. Rifle, shotgun, assault
weapon, large- and small-bore handguns . . .
I'd had all of those aimed in my direction at
one time or another, and the sensation was
always the same. Cold clenching in the gut.
Every sense suddenly heightened, nerves
and muscles bowstring taut. Adrenaline
rush of fear that you immediately fight
down and control, because you know the
worst thing you can do is let it take hold
and escalate into panic. All of that happens
inside. Outwardly you show none of it, do
the same thing you would if you were being
menaced by a vicious animal: stand dead
still, maintain a blank expression without
challenge or bravado, keep a clear head to
give yourself time to assess the situation and
figure a way out of it.

Five or six seconds passed while I looked
alternately at Haxner and the gun, gauging

my chances. Not good. There were a dozen feet of carpet and the edge of a coffee table separating us, and the gun was big and steady in his hand. Looked like a Glock 9mm automatic — a weapon with a muzzle velocity that could do the same kind of damage to a man's head as Canaday's .41 Magnum. The only possible advantage I had was the dusky light in the room, and he took that away by reaching behind him with his free hand and flicking on the ceiling globe.

He said in a flat, bitter voice, "Looks like I caught myself a snoop."

Without moving, I put on what I hoped was a sheepish expression. He was in full uniform, so I said, "You working a different shift at Bayfront today?"

"Same shift. I was there until Krikowski told me about you, then I figured I'd better come back home. Lucky for me I did."

Damn Krikowski. And damn me for taking it on faith that he'd keep his mouth shut. "I didn't break in. The front door was unlocked."

"Like hell it was."

"You just came in that way. Wasn't locked, was it?"

He didn't say anything. The gun moved slightly in his hand.

"Check the other doors and the windows,"

I said. "You won't find any breakage or jimmy marks. I just walked in."

Still had nothing to say.

"Stupid thing to do, I admit it. But all I did was look around — didn't disturb or take anything."

"Making a hell of a lot of noise when I came in. Sounded like you were moving furniture around. Find what you were looking for?"

"No. Nothing to find."

Haxner's uniform cap was bothering him in some way; he jerked it off and tossed it in the direction of the sofa. It was the first time I'd seen him without it. Close-cropped graying hair covered a bullet-shaped skull, and there were patchy knots of gristle at the edges of his forehead, on his cheekbones, and around his jawline. Hard man, ugly by most standards, and maybe that was the appeal he'd had for Verity Daniels — a hunk of raw meat after the pabulum of Vincent Canaday.

I said, "So what happens now?"

"What you think happens now?"

"You either call the police and have me arrested for trespassing, or I apologize and you let me walk out of here and we forget the whole thing."

It was a few seconds before he said, "Uh-

uh. I come home, find you going through my house, you jump me and I shoot you in self-defense."

"Why would you want to do that? I told you, I didn't find anything incriminating."

"Yeah, you told me."

"Search me if you think otherwise."

"Smart guy, too smart to take anything with you. Leave it here, bring in the cops, let them find it."

Haxner was talking about the jewelry hidden in the headboard. Maybe the bloodstains, too. The plastic sheeting and rope in the garage hadn't occurred to him as incriminating or he'd have gotten rid of them by now.

I said, "You don't have anything to lose by letting me walk out of here. Get rid of whatever it is you think I found, and it'd be your word against mine. The police couldn't touch you."

"You must think I'm stupid. How do I know what else you know?"

"Nobody's going to buy a self-defense claim. Unarmed man my age, with forty years in law enforcement."

"Take my chances."

The sweaty tension in him was palpable. He knew how to handle a firearm and he was probably a good shot, but there was nothing in his record to indicate he'd ever fired a weapon in the line of duty, either as a cop or a security guard; and shooting at a target and putting a bullet in a man looking you in the eye are two different things. He was capable of it, but it wouldn't be easy for him. He'd have to nerve himself up to it.

Keep him talking. If I couldn't talk him out of it, maybe he'd lose what nerve he had and do it himself. And if not . . . take careful baby steps forward and to my right, away from the coffee table, whenever his attention wavered slightly. If it came down to having to rush him, I had to be as close as I could get to have any chance at all.

"The way things stand now," I said, "a smart lawyer could plea bargain the Verity Daniels killing down to second degree, maybe even to manslaughter. But two murders . . . that's first degree for sure."

"Bullshit. Nobody could prove anything with you dead."

"Sure they could. Krikowski's not the only one who knows I've been investigating you. My partner knows — and she knows I'm here. You going to shoot her, too?"

No response.

"Then there's your neighbors. I talked to half a dozen before I came in here. You think none of them ever saw you with Verity Daniels?"

"You're lying," Haxner said. "You never talked to the neighbors."

"Woman in the house across the street: Latina, about forty, mole on her left cheek. Man in the house next door: pushing seventy, bald, scraggly white beard, not too friendly —"

"All right, so you're not lying. Doesn't change anything."

"Sure it does. I've been in the neighborhood nearly two hours now, asking questions about you, and my car's parked right out front. Add that to what my partner knows, what Krikowski knows, what I told you about my age and reputation. Think about it, Haxner."

He thought about it, the gristly knots on his face bunching and rippling. "Then I'll have to do it another way."

"There isn't any other way."

"Yeah, there is."

Pretty obvious what he was thinking. Tie me up, bring his car into the garage and load me into the trunk, drive to some remote place and shoot me there. Stupid idea. But if he thought that was his only way out, he'd try it. Only I was not about to let it happen. If I was going to take a bullet

329

from that Glock, it would be right here in this house.

I eased another tiny step forward while he was thinking it over. Then I said, "Why did you kill her?"

". . . What?"

"Verity Daniels. No reason now not to tell me."

A little silence. Then, "Goddamn it, I didn't mean to. It wasn't my fault."

It's never their fault, the Haxners of the world. It's always the victims' — lovers, family members, friends, strangers, gang rivals, some poor bastard being robbed or assaulted. Always the victims who did something to provoke them into pulling the trigger, picking up the knife, raising the blunt instrument, using their fists or their squeezing fingers.

"She was crazy," he said. "Crazy woman. I never should've got mixed up with her."

"Why did you?"

"How many chances you think a guy like me has with a rich young piece? She put it out there, I took it. Christ, she was wild in bed. Do anything and everything." The ghost of a smile. "Always wanted to get on top. Called it being on her guard."

"Yeah," I said. "One of her little games."

"Had to make a goddamn game out of

everything she did. Wouldn't just come here on her own, use the spare key I got for her. No, we had to meet somewhere, have breakfast, have lunch, then I'd have to drive her here and drive her back to her car. Like we were trying to fool somebody. Who the hell cared if I was banging her? Nobody except my bosses and I wouldn't've done it in her condo if she'd wanted me to."

The spare key had to be the one I'd found in the urn. Daniels must have put it there on the sly without telling Haxner. "The extortion hoax was even crazier. Why'd you go along with it?"

"I didn't. Didn't know what she was up to until it was too late."

"You must have had some idea. You're the one who told her about Baker Beach and Lands End, right?"

"Yeah. But then she wanted me to make some anonymous phone calls, pretend I was trying to threaten money out of her. Part of a little harmless fun she was planning to have, she said. Harmless fun. Christ! I told her I didn't play those kinds of games. Pissed her off, so she clammed up afterward." The facial knots bunched and rippled again. "I never knew Runyon was a PI until the night he flashed his ID and asked me about building security. Or what the hell was going on when the cops showed up. Wasn't until the next day that I got the truth out of her."

"But you went right on seeing her, helping her. Why?"

"Promised me money, ten thousand bucks, more if the lawsuits paid off. I never had that much cash in my life. Now I never will."

"So you killed her before she paid off."

"Told you, it wasn't my fault. Damn bitch went psycho on me — I had to protect myself."

"What made her go psycho?"

"Runyon's coat button. Little thing like that. We're in bed, she tells me she found it the night before in her condo, must've got torn off when she was wrestling with him. She had it in her purse. Showed it to me, all excited. Said she couldn't decide whether to take it to the cops right away or wait and spring it at the trial. I told her forget it, don't run any more crazy risks. She didn't like that. Went off on me all of a sudden like she did when something didn't go her way, only twice as batshit . . . yelling, calling me dirty names. Next thing I know she's all over me, scratching, biting, trying to break my balls. Crazy woman attacks you like that, you fight back. I smacked her, she grabbed the lamp off the nightstand and tried to brain me, I got it away from her . . . but she still wouldn't quit. . . ."

"So you hit with it and then choked her."

"I don't remember much about that," Haxner lied. He remembered, all right, and he didn't like the images that had come crawling into his mind; his free hand lifted to finger his throat. "She had me as crazy as she was by then . . . I just lost it."

"Leaving you with a dead body on your hands. So you came up with the bright idea of stripping off her jewelry —"

"That's enough, shut up." The memories were still plaguing him; he kept on rubbing his throat.

"— and putting the button in her hand to lay the blame on Runyon, then you went and got her car and brought it back here —"

"I said, shut up!" He came forward a couple of steps, jabbing with the Glock. "Turn around, walk into the kitchen."

"Suppose I don't?"

"I'll drop you where you stand. You got five seconds."

He meant it. He was nerved up enough now; guilt and fear had pushed him right to the edge. There was a darkness in his face,

like a chunk of sky roiled with thunder-
heads.

I turned and moved. The only chance I
had was in another place — the kitchen, the
garage. If he got close enough, careless
enough, I might be able to jump him. If he
didn't, I'd have to make a move anyway. I
was not about to let him tie me up. Nobody
was ever going to tie me up again.

There was nothing I could grab for a
weapon in the dining room or the kitchen,
and Haxner hung back far enough anyway
so that I didn't dare make any sudden
moves. The garage was where we were going. The door to it opened inward and I
thought I might have a chance to catch hold
of its edge going through and swing it back
between us, but he was wise to that. He told
me to open it as far as it would go, leave it
like that, then go into the garage with my
hands together behind my back. I did that,
so stiff with tension now that it felt as if I
were moving through semisolid matter.

Once I was onto the concrete floor, Haxner ordered me to move to my left and then
stop. When I complied, I heard him step
down and then sidle off in the opposite
direction. I made a slow half-turn — would
have turned even if he'd told me not to —
so I could see where he was headed. On his

way to the workbench in a sidewise walk, watching me with the Glock extended back in my direction.

I stood still then except for little head movements and eye shifts. I was a couple of steps from the inner wall and a row of dusty, sagging shelves that stretched along it. The only items the shelves held were a plastic bucket, a pair of rusty hedge clippers out of my reach, and half a dozen topless coffee cans. Inside one of the cans on a lower shelf was what looked to be a jumble of old faucet parts.

Haxner was at the bench now, reaching up for a roll of duct tape hanging on a hook.

I looked at the wall again. And when I saw the electric push-button between the end of the shelving and the doorjamb, I knew what I was going to do. Instant decision: there was no time to consider it and I might never have another chance.

Haxner's fingers closed around the tape roll. He fumbled it a little as he pulled it off the hook; his gaze flicked away from me for an instant. I sucked in a breath and made my move — fast sliding step to my right, hard jab on the push-button with my left thumb. The overhead door mechanism was old and the sudden grinding noise of the gears made Haxner jerk and lose his focus, just long enough for me to snatch up the coffee can and throw it at him as I lunged forward.

He ducked, triggered a round at the same instant the can hit the wall behind him and peppered him with the faucet parts. Wild shot, the boom of it adding to the racket of the door going up. Haxner bellowed something and squeezed off another round that didn't quite miss: I felt the sting of the bullet on my left forearm. And then I was on him.

I got my hand around the hot squared barrel of the gun and tore it out of his hand, but I couldn't hold it; the weapon went banging and skidding across the floor. I wrapped my arms around him, twisted him away from the bench. He had twenty years on me, but I had more experience and the benefit of adrenaline-driven fury. When he couldn't break loose, he tried to rupture me; I turned in time, took the thrust on my upper thigh, and retaliated by stomping down hard on his instep. That ripped loose another yell, hurt him enough to buckle his knees. He pulled me with him when he went down.

That was all right because I landed on top, full weight, slamming his head into the concrete. He grunted, moaned, but the fight didn't go out of him. He bucked me half off, forced me to roll with him — out through the open garage door onto the driveway. I came up on top again, reared back to get leverage, and hit him twice, right fist, left fist. The first was a glancing blow because I was half blind with sweat; the second landed solidly on his knotted jaw-line, with enough force behind it to smack his head into the pavement again. And that ended it. He went limp under me.

I crawled off him, knelt for a few seconds with my head down to catch my breath. An idiotic urge to laugh came over me. Old man fighting like a school kid . . . fighting for his life. Damn wonder I hadn't died of a heart attack, if not from one of the slugs he'd pumped at me.

The thought made me aware of the sting-ing in my arm. I wiped my eyes clear to look at the damage. The bullet had torn through my coat and shirt sleeves, but there wasn't much blood. Flesh wound. My lucky day.

A man was standing on the sidewalk, I re-alized then, staring goggle-eyed. When he saw me looking at him, he ran off across the street as if he thought I might start chasing him. There was nobody else around except for Haxner, moving his arms and legs now in a series of twitches, his eyes rolled up in his head. Concussion, I thought, and the thought made me happy — but only for as long as it took to go back into the garage, pick up the Glock, and then call 911.

EPILOGUE

JAKE RUNYON

It was a long five days after Bill's confrontation with George Haxner before they released him. Bill had to do a lot of explaining, Haxner was in the hospital with a severe head injury and couldn't be questioned, the homicide inspectors had to do a preliminary investigation and then convince a judge to issue a search warrant, and the forensics people had to be prodded into doing a rush analysis of the bloodstains and other evidence found in Haxner's home. Plus there was the weekend sandwiched in between to slow things down even more.

Eventually the DA's office dropped the charges, notified the judge of the dismissal, and when the judge in turn dismissed the charge in writing, Runyon was officially off the hook. He signed the release papers, and they gave him back his personal possessions. His laptop, too, which they'd confiscated.

When he walked out with Dragovich, Bill and Tamara were waiting. Bryn wasn't there because she hadn't been told exactly when he was being released. No need for her to endure another trip to the Hall of Justice. The one time she'd visited him, she'd been supportive but uncomfortable: too many bad memories of her own time trapped behind bars.

Tamara suggested the four of them go somewhere, have a drink and kick back a little, but he begged off; it would only have turned into a rehash session and he wasn't feeling sociable to begin with. They understood without much being said.

Bill drove him to the AutoReturn offices at 450 Seventh Street, the city's vehicle impound facility, where he had to pay nearly a thousand dollars to ransom his Ford, the police having impounded it to search for bloodstains and other evidence that wasn't there. But their apology didn't include a waiver of the usual towing and storage fees. The city bureaucracy didn't operate that way. Separate agencies, the SFPD and AutoReturn, which in his case translated to separate screwings.

Runyon shook hands with Bill in the storage lot, thanked him again for all he'd done, and they went their separate ways. He drove up over Twin Peaks and down to his apartment. The place had a musty, closed-up smell; he opened a couple of windows to air it out. The police hadn't made a mess in their search of the premises, but then they hadn't been too careful about it, either. He straightened up, put some things back where they belonged. Then he took a long, hot shower, shaved, dressed in clean clothes, and sat down in the living room to call Bryn and tell her he was out.

"Oh, Jake," she said, "I'm so relieved. Are you okay?"

"I will be."

"Why don't you come over for dinner tonight? Bobby would love to see you. We'll celebrate."

Celebrate. Getting sprung from jail when you were innocent of the charge that put you there wasn't a cause for celebration. Bryn ought to remember that; she hadn't wanted festivities last spring any more than he did now.

"Rain check," he said. "I've got some catching up to do here."

"I understand. Tomorrow, then, or whenever you'd like. But soon."

"Soon."

"Just give me a little advance notice. I'll cook something special."

"Sure. That'll be great."

He booted up his laptop to see if any of the settings had been fouled up by SFPD's computer people. No, they were all okay. He checked his e-mail. Not many messages, considering the amount of time he'd been locked up, and none that required immediate attention.

The apartment was cold now; he shut the windows. Then he put on his jacket and went out to the Ford and started driving. Going nowhere in particular, just out of the city — a long way out of the city. Daylight ride that would turn into a night ride, maybe a late-night ride.

Once he was into it, he finally felt free again.

TAMARA

She almost didn't answer the doorbell.

Last time it had rung unexpectedly it'd been Antoine Delman and a big load of trouble. More trouble this time, too, if not the deadly kind, because she had a feeling who was standing out there on the front stoop. Couldn't have said how or why, just that she knew as soon as she heard the bell.

Go away, nobody home.

Bell went off again. And again.

Knows I'm home, she thought. All right,

then. Have to deal with him eventually, might as well be now.

She went downstairs, opened the door on the heavy-duty chain she'd had installed. And yeah, there he was. Smiling in the old wistful way he had, those big brown eyes of his round and bright as a stuffed bear's. Big as a bear, too. Hair shorter than she remembered it and starting to recede a little in front (good!). Dressed in a sport jacket and a pair of slacks, as if spiffing up would make a difference to her.

"Hello, Tam."

"So it's you. How'd you find out where I live?"

"Wasn't too hard. We still have some mutual friends."

"Tell me which one and it'll be one less of mine."

"You look good," he said. Eating her up with those brown eyes, damn him. "You've lost weight, I can tell from your face. Don't mind my saying, it makes you even more attractive."

"None of your sweet-talk crap. What do you want?"

"Talk to you, that's all."

"I don't have the Toyota anymore. Told you that on the phone."

"Yes, you do — I saw it parked down the

343

block. But that's not why I'm here. I've got another car now."

"Thought you didn't have any money. What'd you do, steal it?"

"Borrowed enough from Charley Phillips's folks to buy a junker. They helped me get a job, too. It's not much — waiter in a Pier Thirty-Nine restaurant — but it'll do until I can find a music gig."

"You think I care?"

"Can I come in? Just for a few minutes?"

"No. Said everything we had to say to each other on the phone."

"No, we didn't. At least I didn't — there's a lot more I want to say to you. I won't stay long, promise."

"Both know what your promises are worth."

He winced. "I know how badly I hurt you and you have every right to tell me to go to hell. All I'm asking is a chance to do some soul-baring first —"

"I don't want to hear it."

"Please, Tam."

"No."

He kept looking at her with those big brown eyes. "Please."

I hate you, you son of a bitch, she thought.

She closed the door — but only far enough so that she could take off the chain. And dammit, *dammit,* when Horace came in past her, the nearness and the familiar scent of him sent little shivers up and down her spine.

BILL

The bullet wound in my arm was a setback for Kerry. Just a flesh wound, hardly more than a scratch, but I couldn't hide it from her. And I couldn't lie to her about how and where I'd gotten it and the handful of bruises and contusions because the one thing we never did was lie to each other.

It upset her pretty badly. Made her scared and clingy at first, then angry, then borderline hysterical. She kept saying things like, "My God, you could have been killed. Somebody could have rung the doorbell and told me you were lying dead in some stranger's garage. What's the matter with you, going into that house the way you did? Why do you take such foolish risks?"

She was right, and I admitted it. Then I made the mistake of saying it wouldn't happen again.

"You said that the last time, and the time before that, and the time before that. It will happen again if you keep putting yourself in harm's way. You have to stop. You have to stop! If you don't, you'll end up killing us both."

". . . What do you mean?"

"You told me after what happened in July you couldn't stand losing me. Well, don't you think I feel the same about you? If I lost you, I couldn't go on, I wouldn't want to go on. Not even for Emily's sake."

"Don't say that. . . ."

"It's the truth. I love Emily, we both do, but it's different with you and me. We're not just married, we're fused together, a single entity. Destroy one half and the other half will die, too. You feel the same, I know you do."

"Of course I do —"

"Then promise me there'll be no more risks, no more deliberate exposure to violence, that I'll never have to worry about you that way again. Promise me! Swear to me!"

"I promise," I said. "I swear."

She looked into my eyes for a long time, as if trying to assure herself that I was sincere. Then she said, "Oh, God, I love you," and threw her arms around me and started to weep.

She was better after that, but the negative effects lingered. Periods of withdrawal, nightmares, crying jags — not as bad as before, but bad enough to erode some of the progress she'd made before my part in the Verity Daniels fiasco. Inadvertently, I'd made her vulnerable again, fearful again. And it was up to me to undo the damage, work harder to renew her healing process.

So I'm home now where I belong, seeing to Kerry's needs, and Emily's, pretty much twenty-four seven. What little work I do for Tamara and the agency is mostly on a consultancy basis. Maybe eventually I'll go back to South Park a couple of days a week now and then, and maybe I won't. If so, it won't be until after Kerry is completely herself again. One thing is for certain: I'll never do any more field work that has even the remotest possibility of danger.

My sworn promise to Kerry is an unbreakable covenant.

I'm out of harm's way for good.